CAN THE SADDLE CLUB GIRLS BEAT THEIR BOYFRIENDS?

As the members of The Saddle Club took their seats on the floor of Max's office, the director of Pine Hollow Stables began his explanation of the upcoming event. "A 'know-down' is a little like a spelling bee," he began. "You'll get to test your knowledge of horses by answering your questions—from one to four points."

Max went on to explain that if they wanted to win the Know-Down, they were going to have to learn a lot of information. "Study hard," he said. "Two weeks from today at our next unmounted meeting, we'll have the Know-Down."

Carole and Stevie exchanged glances. Two weeks from now was when their boyfriends, Cam and Phil, were coming to their Pony Club meeting!

"Egad," Stevie whispered. "What are we going to do?"

Carole leaned over and whispered quietly into Stevie's ear. "Win," she said.

THE SADDLE CLUB

STABLE MANNERS

BONNIE BRYANT

A BANTAM SKYLARK BOOK®
NEW YORK · TORONTO · LONDON · SYDNEY · AUCKLAND

RL 5, 009–012

STABLE MANNERS

A Bantam Skylark Book / June 1993

ISBN 0-553-48075-8

Published simultaneously in the United States and Canada

PRINTED IN THE UNITED STATES OF AMERICA

CWO   0 9 8 7 6 5 4 3 2 1

STABLE MANNERS

"DID YOU DO it?" Stevie asked.

"Hm-hmmm. Did you?" Carole replied.

"Yup," said Stevie.

"Is he coming?" Stevie asked.

"Hm-hmmm," Carole replied. "And what about Phil?"

"Yup," said Stevie.

"Oh, how great!" Lisa said, her eyes sparkling with excitement for her friends.

The threesome, Stevie Lake, Carole Hanson, and Lisa Atwood, were all walking together toward their favorite place in the world, Pine Hollow. That was the riding stable where they all took lessons and be-

1

longed to a Pony Club called Horse Wise together. Now, it seemed, there was going to be something extra special going on.

At the last Horse Wise meeting, the director, a man named Max Regnery who was also the girls' riding instructor and the owner of Pine Hollow, had reminded the Pony Club members that they could invite friends to any unmounted meeting. An unmounted meeting was one in which the members would not be on horseback. They had unmounted meetings every other week. When Max had said that, Carole had told Stevie she should invite Phil Marsten. Phil was Stevie's boyfriend and he belonged to the Cross County Pony Club. Stevie had immediately replied that she'd invite Phil if Carole would invite Cam.

Cam Nelson was a boy Carole had met when they competed against one another in a horse show. Actually, Carole had sort of met Cam before then because they both belonged to the same computer bulletin board and they'd been sending notes to one another. The funny thing was, Carole had assumed that Cam was a girl before seeing him in person at the horse show. It turned out that he was a really nice guy and they liked one another a lot. Inviting Cam to the Horse Wise meeting seemed like the perfect way to

2

see him again, but she was nervous about it. Carole tended to be a little bit shy where boys were concerned and she didn't want to appear too eager.

"Cam was really nice about it," Carole said. "He said yes right away. Then he asked his mother and father. The first thing he said, though, was yes."

Stevie clapped Carole on the back gently. "My dear," she said. "You have so much to learn."

"I do?" Carole asked. She thought she'd been learning a lot.

"Number one rule is that when a boy calls you three times a week, he's going to say yes when you invite him to something."

"I hadn't thought about that," Carole said. But she was still thinking about it—and liking what she was thinking—when they walked up the gravel driveway to Pine Hollow.

"Let's check on the mare before Horse Wise starts," Lisa suggested. That seemed like a good idea, so the three of them hurried into the locker area, put their sandwiches into their cubbies, and headed for the foaling box.

Max had recently acquired a stallion named Geronimo for Pine Hollow so he could do some breeding. It meant that mares would sometimes now come to the stable to have their foals so they could be bred soon after they'd given birth. The girls thought that was very exciting and hoped they'd have lots of chances to see births and newborn foals.

Although Stevie, Lisa, and Carole were very different from one another, they shared something so important that it transcended all their differences. They loved horses. They loved them so much that they had formed their very own group called The Saddle Club. There were only two requirements for membership. First of all, members had to be horse crazy. The second was that they had to be willing to help one another out, no matter what the problem. Both of those were easy requirements for the girls. They'd gotten one another out of all kinds of trouble. That had included jams having to do with horses and riding and it had included other things, too—schoolwork, boyfriends, family trouble. Their most recent adventure had even led straight down the aisle—to a wedding! They sometimes got the feeling there wasn't anything they couldn't do when they worked together.

The girls greeted the mare with gentle pats. She seemed sort of edgy, not as friendly as she had been the day before.

"Do you think that means something?" Lisa asked.

"It probably means she's in a bad mood," Stevie reasoned.

"Isn't that the sign that the foal is coming? Like really soon?" Lisa asked. This time she looked at Carole, who was bound to give a more detailed answer.

Carole shrugged. "Stevie could be right. Or she might be a little colicky. That's common in mares who are near term. She could also be about to foal. The vet will be here later. We can mention it to her."

"We *should* mention it to her, you mean," Lisa said. She was becoming more and more convinced that she had spotted something that meant the mare was about to have her foal and she wanted her friends to agree.

"Yes, right, we *should*," Carole said.

"We *should* also be getting into Max's office now," Stevie said pointedly. "It's almost time for the meeting to begin."

The girls gave the mare a final pat—or tried to. Instead she backed away from their affectionate touches. They left her in peace and headed for Horse Wise.

Most unmounted meetings began in Max's office where he would explain what the rest of the meeting was going to be about. The girls quickly spotted a large stack of papers on his desk. That meant there was going to be some kind of a handout. Stevie's eyes were good and, being the kind of girl she was, she was an expert at reading upside down.

"What did it say?" Carole asked, taking a seat cross-legged on the floor among the rest of the Horse Wise members.

"Something about bowing down," Stevie said, crinkling her forehead because it didn't make sense even to her.

"Bowing down?"

"Bow-down, how-down—something like that."

Carole and Lisa shrugged. For once, it appeared that Stevie was wrong and they were just going to have to wait to find out.

As it happened, Stevie wasn't all that wrong at all. As soon as the meeting began, Max picked up the pile of papers and began handing them out to everyone. At the top of the first page, it said "Know-Down."

"See?" Stevie said proudly.

"Shhhhhh," Max said. "No talking, as you know, Ms. Lake."

She took her papers and glanced at them quickly.

"I don't want you looking at these now," Max said. "You have two weeks to look at them. So, for now, just fold them and put them aside."

"But what are they for?" Stevie asked.

"And while you're folding them and putting them aside, I'll tell you what they're for," Max said. He glared a little at Stevie. As she well knew, he didn't

6

like to be interrupted. He liked to tell things in his own time. Stevie got the hint. She and her friends folded their sheets of paper and held them on their laps.

Then Max began his explanation. "A 'know-down' is a little bit like a spelling bee," he began. "You'll get the chance to test your knowledge of horses by answering questions. And each of you will be able to choose the difficulty of your questions—from one to four points. A four-point question might have four parts to the answer, like, for instance, 'Name the parts of a horse's back between the shoulder and the dock.'"

"Withers, back, loins, croup!" Stevie called out excitedly.

"And with that answer, you'd get four points," Max said. "Except that unless you raise your hand, I'm not going to give you any credit."

Stevie grimaced.

"And besides, the Know-Down hasn't started, so you've just provided the answer to the first four-point question to everyone else," he said.

Stevie raised her hand. Max called on her.

"Sorry," she said. He smiled and accepted her apology. Stevie seemed to have ways of getting out of hot water that were as smooth as the ways she slipped into it.

Max went on to explain that they would be able to choose easier questions worth fewer points, but if they wanted to win the Know-Down, they were going to have to learn a lot of information.

"It's all there," he said. "Study hard. Two weeks from today at our next unmounted meeting, we'll have the Know-Down."

Carole and Stevie exchanged glances. Two weeks from now was when Phil and Cam were coming to the meeting! Carole could feel a little knot tying itself in the center of her stomach. She'd been eager to have Cam come to the meeting when she thought it was just going to be a regular meeting, but this wasn't going to be regular. It was almost like a test. She wouldn't mind if Cam did a little bit better than she did and she didn't think Cam would mind if she did a little bit better than he did, but what if she blew it and made a fool of herself? Would Cam ever want to talk to her again? Cam loved horses as much as she did. What would he think of her if she did badly?

Maybe she could call Cam and cancel. She could say that the meeting had been postponed or was going to be a mounted meeting, or she'd gotten the date wrong, or she was going to have to be away that week-end, or anything at all. Then, as Carole thought about that for a minute, trying to decide which excuse she'd use, she realized she wasn't being fair. Cam would probably love participating in a Know-Down. It was totally out of the question to uninvite him, no matter what reason she came up with or how good it sounded or how nervous she might be. And since he would be there, there was only one thing to do: study. She clutched the folded sheets tightly.

"Egad," Stevie whispered. "What are we going to do?"

Carole leaned over and whispered quietly into her ear. "Win," she said.

Stevie grinned. This was something she could understand. From the very beginning of her friendship with Phil, they'd been in competition on the subject of horses and riding. It seemed that whenever they were together, one was trying to prove better than the other. For a while, Stevie had taken it very seriously. That had almost been the end of her friendship with Phil. Then she'd learned that, most of the time, the two of them could compete and have fun and in the end that was what was most important. Of course Stevie would certainly try to win. And so would Phil. That was a nice part about their friendship: It brought out the best in each of them. That was the way Stevie felt most of the time. Other times, however, she just couldn't help herself and it seemed like being better than Phil was the most important thing in the world.

"Definitely," Stevie agreed.

"Ahem, did you say something?" Max asked, glaring at Stevie.

"No, it was me," Lisa said, saving both of her whispering friends. "Sorry, but I should have raised my hand." She raised her hand and Max called on her.

"We checked the mare before we came in here and she seems edgy. Doesn't that mean she's about to foal?" Lisa asked.

"Maybe," Max said. "It could also mean nothing. Judy made her daily vet check yesterday and didn't seem concerned. She'll be back this afternoon and will check again."

"But I know that when a mare gets edgy, it's a sign that she's about to foal," Lisa persisted.

"It can be," Max agreed. "There are other signs, too. Does anybody know what they are?"

Hands started going up. Max got a lot of answers to the question and he told the pony clubbers that they were all right. Different mares apparently had a lot of different indicators that they were near term.

"So, it seems that the only way to be sure that a mare is about to begin serious labor is when serious labor begins," Max said. "It's just not a simple question."

Lisa found herself a little annoyed, as she had been with her friends. She was used to being right. She was an excellent student who got straight A's. She didn't think Max or her friends were paying enough attention to this strong indicator that the mare was about to foal and she was confident that the mare would soon prove her right. *That'll show everyone I know what I'm talking about,* she thought smugly.

Soon the meeting broke for lunch, scheduled to reconvene in the feed room, where they'd get a lesson on blending feed grains.

Lisa was heading for the door when she heard Max call her name. He also called another rider, a much younger girl named May Grover. Lisa thought he probably wanted to apologize to her for correcting her about the mare, but she found that he had something else on his mind.

"I want you two to work together on something," Max said. "I'm going to start a Big Sister/Little Sister learning program and you're my test case."

For a moment Lisa forgot about the mare. This sounded interesting.

"One of the things we rarely have time for here," Max went on, "is working with hitching horses and

11

ponies to carts and wagons. It's just something we don't do much and that's too bad because it's fun. Lisa, I want you to take this book"—he handed Lisa a small paperback—"and learn how to do it yourself and teach May to do it. Then in ten days, after the Tuesday class, I'd like the two of you to do a demonstration for the rest of Horse Wise. Will you have time to work on this together? You can use Nickel and hitch him to the cart we use for pony rides sometimes. Then, if you'd like, you can take the Horse Wise members for rides."

Lisa looked at May. The young girl's eyes were as big as saucers. Lisa herself wasn't so excited. For one thing, preparing for the Know-Down was going to be a lot of work. For another thing, rides in pony carts seemed very tame compared to all the other wonderful things you could do with a horse. And then there was the mare. She was about to foal and Lisa seemed to be the only one who knew it. That was a big responsibility in itself.

"Lisa?" Max asked. He seemed a little surprised by her hesitation.

Lisa gulped. Even if she wanted to, how could she say no?

"Sure," she agreed finally, looking lamely at the book in her hand. She flipped through it. It wasn't very long. She'd be able to get through it. What could possibly be involved in hitching a pony to a wagon? The pictures in the book showed a very little girl doing the work. May could probably do most of this all by herself. Lisa would just be there to help. "No problem," Lisa said.

"I WONDER WHAT Max wanted to talk to Lisa about," Carole said to Stevie.

"Me, too, but whatever it is, I'm glad he's got her for a few minutes."

"Why?" Carole asked.

"We have to talk," Stevie said, pulling her sandwich out of her cubby. She signaled Carole to join her and the two of them found a clean empty stall where they could talk privately for a few minutes.

"What's up?" Carole was really curious. It wasn't like Stevie to have something to talk about that didn't include Lisa.

"It has to do with the Know-Down," said Stevie.

14

"Oh, sure. We're going to have to work like crazy and we'll need Lisa's help, won't we?"

"We will," Stevie agreed. "But that's not what I mean. The problem is that we each have a boyfriend coming to it and Lisa doesn't. She's kind of left out on that."

"She doesn't seem to mind," Carole said.

"Of course she doesn't *seem* to mind," said Stevie. "We're best friends. She's not going to make us feel uncomfortable by letting us know that she minds, because we're such good friends. But I'm sure she does mind. Even if it's only a little."

Carole thought about it for a minute. The truth was, she didn't quite think of Cam as a boyfriend. He was a really nice guy she'd met once and talked to a lot, but they hadn't had a date or anything. He'd held her hand for a few minutes when they took a walk after the horse show. That had been nice, but did it mean he was a boyfriend? Carole finally decided that even if she wasn't ready to call Cam her boyfriend, Lisa probably would see him that way.

"Okay," Carole agreed.

The girls bit into their sandwiches and were silent for a few minutes as they contemplated the Know-Down that was coming up.

"I'm really nervous about having Cam there," Car-

15

ole admitted. "What if he knows more than me?" She paused. "Or what if *I* know more than him?" She threw up her hands.

Stevie grinned at her friend's distress. "I know what you mean. But I've decided that it doesn't matter if we beat them or not. The only thing that matters is learning more about horses. That's the whole purpose of the thing."

Carole raised her eyebrows. That didn't sound like competitive Stevie.

"I'm serious," Stevie reassured her.

"I totally agree," Carole said. "So we should send these study sheets to Phil and Cam so we don't have an unfair advantage."

"Of course," said Stevie. "Let's borrow envelopes and stamps from Mrs. Reg right now and put these in the mail. We can make copies of Lisa's study sheets at your house tonight."

"Sure. Our next-door neighbor has a copying machine and she's always telling Dad and me we can use it."

The girls wrapped up their half-eaten sandwiches and headed for Mrs. Reg's office. Mrs. Reg was Max's mother and the stable manager. Her desk was a confusion of organization. There were papers everywhere, but they were carefully organized. That was like Mrs.

16

Reg. Everything seemed out of place, but when it was examined, there was always an underlying logic.

"Envelopes here," Stevie said, reaching into the lowest drawer.

"And stamps here," Carole said, locating a roll of stamps in the corner of the top drawer.

"And a pen?" Stevie searched the top of the desk and found Mrs. Reg's pen on top of some order forms she was probably about to take care of.

It only took a minute for each girl to scribble a note and address the envelope to her friend. There was a mailbox out in front of the stable. Stevie took their letters, walked them out to the street, and dropped them in the mailbox while Carole went in search of Lisa.

LISA WAS TRYING to be patient, but it wasn't easy. Where she wanted to be was checking on the mare again. She thought she'd heard Judy Barker's truck pull into the stable driveway and she wanted to be there when Judy confirmed to Max that the mare was about to foal. Instead Lisa was stuck tromping across a small paddock with May Grover. May had insisted on examining the pony cart and that was kept in a little shed along with a buckboard and a sleigh that Max also had for horses to pull. May had never seen any of them and was excited at the prospect of learning something totally new about Pine Hollow. Lisa had tried to talk her into checking on the mare first, but when May wanted to do something, she could be extremely stubborn. She wanted to see the pony cart.

"This way," Lisa said, leading May to the shed. She was grumbling to herself about it when she felt May take her hand. Suddenly she remembered that May was just a little girl, small enough so that when she crossed streets she still took her mother's hand. It was a simple gesture and it made Lisa feel a certain responsibility to the little girl who was entrusting her hand to Lisa's. Lisa gripped the small hand affectionately.

"Are you excited about the Know-Down?" Lisa asked.

"Am I ever!" said May. "The trouble is, I won't know which to work on harder—the Know-Down or our project."

"You'll find time for it all," Lisa said assuringly. "All you have to do is study your sheets for the Know-Down."

"I know," May said. "I put them in my pocket so I wouldn't lose them . . ." Her voice trailed off.

Then she let go of Lisa's hand and patted her pocket. She patted her other pocket.

"Oh, no!" she said, and the tone of her voice was clear. "I've lost them already!"

"Don't worry," Lisa said. "Max will give you another set. Just ask him when we get back."

"I don't want him to know I lost them," May said. She was clearly distressed and Lisa wanted to comfort her.

"Here, take mine." Lisa pulled the folded papers out of her pocket. "I can borrow one of my friends' and copy them so Max will never know that either of us lost a set, okay?"

"Okay," May said happily. She took Lisa's study sheets and tucked them carefully into her pocket. Lisa hoped May wouldn't lose those, too, but her concern faded when she saw how deeply May pushed them into her pocket.

When they reached the shed, Lisa opened the door and flipped on the light. There, in one corner, was the little pony cart they would be using to hitch Nickel. It was very small compared to the buckboard, which was a full-sized flatbed wagon, and very plain compared to the elaborate, old-fashioned one-horse open sleigh. Although Lisa usually thought that everything that had to do with horses was important, she was struck only by how plain and how small and how totally insignificant the pony cart appeared.

"Wow!" said May. "Look at these things!"

"Come on, let's get back to the stable," said Lisa. "I think I heard Judy's truck arrive."

"Can I sit in the cart, please?" May asked. "Just for a minute?"

Lisa was discovering that it was very hard to say no to May. She gave the little girl a boost into the back of the cart and watched as she sat as proudly as if she were the Queen of the World on her own throne.

"Come on," Lisa urged her. "Let's go."

They couldn't go right then, though, because May just had to try out the buckboard and the sleigh as well. She thought maybe the sleigh was the best of them, but she wasn't sure. She wanted to try the pony cart again.

When the two of them finally headed back to the stable, Lisa watched Judy's truck pull out of the driveway. She'd been there, examined the mare, and moved on before Lisa even had a chance to ask her about the mare's moodiness.

Lisa rushed to the mare's stall and found Carole and Stevie there.

"Where have you been?" Carole asked.

"I've been with May Grover—oh, it's a long story," she said. She didn't want to take the time to explain

20

about their Big Sis/Little Sis project right then. She wanted to know about the mare.

"What did Judy say?" she asked. "Didn't she say that the mare's moodiness meant she's about to foal?"

"Oh, I forgot to ask," Stevie said. "Judy was just here for a minute."

Lisa was irritated that her friends would forget to ask her question.

"But didn't she say the mare could foal at any time?"

"I don't think so," Carole said. "She just checked on her and nodded, like everything seems to be on schedule. She's not due to foal for another two weeks, you know."

Lisa knew. She was also convinced she was right that it wasn't going to be another two weeks. She wished her friends would take her more seriously. Of the three of them, she was the newest rider, but she'd worked very hard and learned everything she could about horses in the relatively short time since her first ride. It didn't seem fair that Stevie and Carole still thought they knew more than she did. Maybe the Know-Down would be an opportunity to show them how much she knew. Of course, by then, there would be a new foal to show them the same thing!

"Horse Wise will resume in five minutes!" a crackling voice announced on the stable's PA system.

"Lunch!" Lisa said, suddenly realizing that she hadn't eaten at all. Carole and Stevie hadn't finished their sandwiches, either. The three of them hurried to the locker area, gobbled their food and drank their juice before returning to the feed room for the second half of the Horse Wise meeting.

"WHERE'S LISA?" CAROLE asked Stevie. The meeting was over and the girls were waiting for Carole's father. He'd been at the Horse Wise meeting because he was a parent volunteer. Now, it seemed, the volunteers were having a meeting of their own and the girls had to wait for that to be over. They didn't mind. Any time spent at Pine Hollow was good time, even if it was spent standing in the driveway. Then, when the volunteers' meeting was over, the three girls were all going to Carole's house for a sleepover. That might even be more fun than the Horse Wise meeting.

"We have to remember not to talk about Cam and Phil too much," Stevie reminded Carole.

"No problem. All we're going to talk about is the Know-Down. There's so much work to do with the study sheets that we won't have time to talk about Cam and Phil. I don't want to hurt Lisa's feelings any more than you do."

"Here she comes," Stevie said. The two of them waved to Lisa as she emerged from the stables. She waved back, then signaled them to come over. They dropped their bags and trotted over to follow Lisa back into the stable.

"Look," she said, when her friends caught up with her at the mare's stall. "She's still cranky and skittish."

Carole observed the mare. She did seem a little frightened. Skittish was definitely the word.

"She's only been here two days and this is an unfamiliar place," Carole reminded Lisa. "Maybe she's just afraid."

"Maybe she's about to have a foal," Lisa said.

"Of course she is," Stevie said. "In about ten days, maybe more. Maybe less."

"Less," Lisa said.

"You girls ready?" That was Colonel Hanson. The parent volunteers' meeting was over and he pulled the car keys out of his pocket.

Lisa gave the mare a last look and sighed. Lisa

24

hated to leave, but there wasn't much she could do about it. By the time she returned to Pine Hollow, there would probably be a foal waiting for her.

"I've got a new one for you, Stevie," Colonel Hanson said, shifting his car into gear while he pulled out onto the road toward home.

"Ready," Stevie said. Her eyes sparkled in anticipation. She and Colonel Hanson shared a love of very bad, very old jokes and they were forever trying to outwit one another with them.

"How can you tell when an elephant's raided your refrigerator?"

"Easy-peasy," Stevie snapped back. "Smell of peanuts on his breath."

"Drat, I thought I had you with that one. All right, then. What has four wheels and flies?"

"A garbage truck. Why don't you try something hard?"

"Hmmmm. Okay. What do you find in the middle of Paris?"

"Eiffel Tower?"

"Nope."

"Right in the middle?"

"Yes, right in the middle."

"That arch thing? The Arc de Triomphe?"

"Nope."

25

Carole joined in. "The Louvre? Place de la Concorde? Notre Dame?"

They tried everything they could remember about Paris, including the Île de la Cité, the Bastille, and Versailles, which, Colonel Hanson was pleased to remind them, was about twenty miles outside of the city. "This is right in the middle of Paris," he said.

"R," said Lisa.

"Are what?" Stevie asked.

"R. It's in the middle of Paris. P-A-R-I-S. R is in the middle," Lisa clarified.

"Very good," said the colonel.

"Groan," said Stevie.

"Da-ad!" Carole complained. Secretly, though, she loved it. She was sure she had the best father in the whole wide world and the fact that her friends seemed to share her opinion always made her feel especially lucky.

Once they solved the colonel's riddle, talk turned to horses. Carole and Stevie were curious about where Lisa had been during lunch. Lisa hadn't had a chance to tell them about the Big Sis/Little Sis project she was doing with May.

"You know, I learned a lot about hitching a horse to a wagon when I was in Vermont," Stevie said. "We used horse-drawn sleighs to collect maple sap."

26

"And I had to hitch the ponies to the cart when we were giving rides at the fair Stevie organized—or rather *dis*organized—last spring. I can help you with it, too."

There was a part of Lisa that was glad for the offer of help from her friends, but there was another part of her that wondered why they always seemed to think they knew so much when she didn't. And then when she *did* know something—like the mare was going to foal any day now—they dismissed it. "Thanks anyway," she said. "But Max said May and I were supposed to work on this together. I guess we'd better leave it that way. You guys will have your chance another time."

Stevie and Carole exchanged glances. It wasn't like Lisa to turn down help, Stevie thought. Lisa *must* be a little jealous of the fact that both Carole and Stevie had boyfriends coming to the Know-Down. She decided that they needed to make Lisa feel included right away. She turned to Carole.

"I can't wait to get to your house so we can start working on the Know-Down together," she said.

"Me, too," Lisa agreed. Stevie was glad to hear that.

"Me, three," Carole added. "In two weeks, we're going to know every single thing on the study sheets."

"We'll knock 'em dead!" Stevie vowed.

At that the threesome shook hands.

Colonel Hanson pulled up into his driveway and the girls piled out of the car and headed for the house. They did want to get to work on their studying, which, since it was about horses, was what they'd want to talk about anyway, but first things first. They needed a snack.

Stevie took the milk out of the refrigerator while Carole located some graham crackers. Lisa found a jar of peanut butter. They were setting out plates, knives, and napkins, including a spot at the table for Colonel Hanson, when he appeared in the kitchen.

"Listen, girls, I have to go out for a while. I had a message on my answering machine. There's a crisis at the office. General Amato is coming for an inspection on Monday and—oh, I won't bore you with details, but it seems I'm needed. I won't be long. Why don't you help yourselves to a snack and I'll be back in about an hour. Leave me some peanut butter, okay?"

"Okay," they agreed, eyeing the jar warily. There was probably enough for all four of them.

"Uh, one other thing," the colonel said. "Carole, I want you to stay away from my desk, okay?"

"Sure, Dad," she said, but she looked puzzled.

"There are some papers there that are kind of private," he explained. "I know you don't go rummaging through my things, but there's some stuff there . . ." He seemed uncomfortable even saying these words.

Then Carole smiled in understanding. "No problem," she assured him.

The colonel saluted, then left the girls to their feast at the kitchen table.

Once each had smeared an ample amount of peanut butter on a graham cracker and managed to down the first bite and chase it with milk, talk began, though slowly until the peanut butter cleared.

"Okay, now the Know-Down. Let's start," Carole said. Then she remembered that she and Stevie had sent their study sheets to Phil and Cam. "Have you got the sheets?" she asked Lisa.

"I had to give mine to May," Lisa said. "She lost her own in what must be record time. Less than five minutes, I think. The girl's amazing. Can I borrow one of yours and copy them?"

"Oh, dear," Carole said, distressed. She explained to Lisa what had happened to them.

"What are we going to do?" Stevie asked. It wasn't as if they'd never be able to replace them, but they'd all been counting on this sleepover to begin serious work.

"Dad," Carole said as if it were an answer. "He's a

volunteer. Max had to give a set of the sheets to the volunteers, too, didn't he?"

"Of course," Stevie agreed. "We'll just wait until he gets back."

"He might not be back for hours!" Carole said. "Just think what we could be learning while he's gone."

"But where did he put them?" Lisa asked.

"On his desk, I'm sure," Carole said. "That's where he puts everything."

"And that's where we're not supposed to go," Lisa reminded her.

"Oh, he doesn't mean that," Carole said.

"I thought he was pretty clear," said Lisa. "He told you not to look on his desk."

Carole smiled at her friends. "He told *me* not to look on his desk. He didn't say anything about you guys. Didn't you get that? See, it's my birthday soon. He's got something on his desk that's supposed to be a surprise for me. I don't know what it is and I really don't want to know, but you can know if you have to. So, the solution is that one of you should go to Dad's desk, find the papers, and then we can go over to Mrs. Jensen's house and copy them on her machine. We'll be back and have the papers on Dad's desk within fifteen minutes. He'll never know and whatever surprise there is for me on his desk, well, you just won't tell me. Okay?" Carole looked to her friends for their agreement.

"I think you've been spending too much time with Stevie," Lisa teased.

The girls laughed. Then, since the whole thing *had* sounded a lot like Stevie Lake's logic, they nominated her to be the one to go to the colonel's desk. Stevie took a final bite of her cracker and peanut butter, a last slug of milk, and headed for the living room where the colonel's desk was.

Stevie didn't feel quite right about this. She thought Carole's father was one of the nicest men in the world and she'd heard what he'd said to Carole and had thought it applied to all of them, not just Carole. On the other hand, there were those who would contend that Stevie was the most curious girl in the world and Stevie wouldn't think of denying it. If there was something interesting about Carole's birthday on her father's desk, Stevie was dying to know what it was.

She turned on the light and walked over to the colonel's desk. Colonel Hanson did everything with a military precision. Stevie's own desk had papers piled high and dripping over the edge onto the floor. Colonel Hanson's desk was completely clear except for a few papers next to the telephone answering machine. Logic told Stevie that those were the papers he'd carried home from Horse Wise and put down next to the answering machine when he'd gotten his message about the problem at the office. There was a pad there where he'd made a notation about the call he'd gotten that had made him hurry back to his office.

Stevie made a mental note about the exact way the papers were lying on the colonel's desk before she touched them. She didn't think he'd worry about fingerprints, but he might notice if anything was out of place. Stevie picked up the papers and was relieved to recognize words that had been typed on Max's old typewriter. At the top it said HORSE WISE KNOW-DOWN. It was just what she was looking for. There were seven sheets of paper, chock-full of information about horses, starting with one-point questions and going up to the four-pointers. The girls were in luck. Now all they had to do was to get the sheets copied and return the originals to the colonel's desk before he got home. She was pretty sure they had time. She hoped she was right. Just to be on the safe side, she turned off the light before returning to the kitchen.

"Bingo!" she declared loudly, walking into the kitchen and rejoining her friends. "Now let's get the rest of this done before your dad gets back. Call your neighbor and see if we can come over now to make the copies."

"Right after you tell me what my father's giving me for my birthday," Carole said.

A mental image of the colonel's desktop flashed into Stevie's mind. It was totally clear. There had been nothing on the desk except the note about the phone call and the Horse Wise papers.

"Nothing," she said.

"I thought I could count on you," Carole teased her.

"I really didn't see anything," said Stevie. "His desk was clear."

"Yeah, yeah," Carole said, nodding. "You're just turning into a Goody Two-Shoes before my eyes. Well, I'll tell you. I don't mind. I honestly *do* like surprises so I'm not going to nag you and I'm not going to look for myself. I've got the best dad in the world and I wouldn't want to ruin his fun anyway."

"Carole—" Stevie began to protest, then she realized that it wouldn't make any difference. Carole was convinced she'd seen something and Stevie wasn't going to be able to change her mind. Carole seemed to like that thought anyway.

Carole hopped down off the kitchen stool and reached for the telephone. In a minute she had Mrs.

Jensen on the phone and the girls had permission to come over and use the copying machine. They scurried next door, made their copies, and hurried back. While Carole and Lisa collated the papers, Stevie returned the colonel's set of Know-Down papers to his desk. Curious, she took another look at his desk. Whether Carole believed her or not, there really was nothing there for her to see. She put the papers back exactly as they had been, turned out the light, and returned to the kitchen.

"Name the parts of a horse between the shoulder and the dock!" Lisa demanded as she entered the room.

"Withers, back, loins, croup," Stevie recited automatically.

"Four points!" Carole declared. That was just the beginning.

AFTER THE GIRLS had been working for a half an hour, Colonel Hanson called to say that the problem at his office was a really big one. He was going to have to be there for a couple of hours and did the girls mind foraging for dinner for themselves.

They didn't mind at all. They all loved Colonel Hanson, but when there were horses to talk about, they might not even notice whether he was there or not.

While Carole flipped the pages of the study sheets and began calling out the next set of questions, Stevie started opening cabinets to find something interesting for dinner.

"What's the difference between a stable bandage and an exercise bandage?" Carole asked.

"It's how high it goes," Lisa said.

"Nope," Carole told her. "Stevie?"

Stevie scrunched her forehead. "It's how low it goes," she said. Carole nodded. "The stable bandage can come down from the hock to the coronet, just above the hoof. The exercise bandage has to stop above the fetlock so the horse can bend his leg."

"Very good," Carole said.

"I remembered it because you asked me the same question five minutes ago," said Stevie. "I guess the trick to winning the Know-Down is going to be hearing all the questions just five minutes before Max asks them."

"Why didn't I remember it?" Lisa asked.

"Well, you sort of remembered it," Stevie said, trying to comfort her a little. "You had the right idea."

"But the wrong answer," said Lisa.

"Don't worry," Carole assured her. "We've just started with these sheets. You'll know everything by the time of the Know-Down."

"I hope so," Lisa said. Although Lisa didn't seem sure of it, her friends certainly were. Lisa was an excellent student and seemed to have an unlimited ability to learn. She might be starting a little bit behind them on some of the information in the sheets, but once she got going, she'd have it all at her fingertips.

"What's appropriate acreage, in general, for a horse who grazes year round?"

"One to two acres per horse," said Lisa.

"Very good," said Carole.

Lisa felt better. She'd been guessing at the amount of land, but it had seemed right and turned out to be. Maybe she would do well at the Know-Down.

"Name the common hand faults in jumping," Carole said. "This is a four-pointer."

"Well, if it includes all the faults Max saw me commit last time I jumped, it's probably a six- or eight-pointer," said Lisa. "But let me try. First I was running my hands up the horse's mane and holding on to it. Then, I wasn't moving my hands enough. He said they were fixed. After that I let them drop alongside the horse's neck and finally he told me I was fiddling. That meant they were moving, but sort of randomly and not with the movement of the horse. I think I made every mistake there is."

"Oh, no," Stevie said to her. "There are a couple of other things you could have done. You could have stuck your elbows out, hiked your hands up as you jumped, lifting them above the horse's neck as if you're trying to lift the horse by the reins, and you could have held your arms straight and stiff so the horse wouldn't get any flex from them at all. You did pretty well without doing those last three."

"And together you get four points on that question," Carole said. "You got every single fault."

"It takes a lot of experience to make that many mistakes at once," Lisa joked.

The girls went on testing one another that way for a while. When they finished the first page of questions, Carole turned over the sheets to Lisa and let her ask. Carole and Stevie assembled something that was a little bit like a meal while they answered questions. Stevie's idea of a meal was some spaghetti with a can of mushrooms and some cream of chicken soup on it. The main advantage of it was that it didn't seem to take very long to cook, once they'd boiled the spaghetti. The disadvantage had to do with the taste because the soup was so thick, but it certainly was filling. They all agreed on that.

The study sheets were carefully organized by point value and within the point values by areas of questions. They all agreed that Max had done a great job, making it easy to study exactly what was going to be asked. There was a lot of material, but a lot of it was already familiar to the girls. They concentrated on the job, but they also had fun.

"What are the most important things to look for in a horse when you are considering buying one?" Stevie asked.

"That's easy," said Carole. "Make sure he's Starlight!"

"Buzzzzzzz! You try it, Lisa."

"First, is he healthy?"

"Right, then next?" Stevie prodded.

"Conformation, meaning are his physical characteristics generally good. That is, do his feet point straight ahead, does his back sway, stuff like that."

"Next?"

"Personality," said Lisa. "He's got to be gentle, friendly, willing, and well-mannered."

"Three points," said Stevie. "Now for the fourth point, what's the least important thing to look for in a horse?"

"Color," said Lisa. "It doesn't matter what his coat looks like, it's his heart that counts."

"Very good," said Stevie. "Now you take over the sheets and test us."

Lisa did. The girls continued working on the study sheets until Colonel Hanson returned from the base. They felt they'd learned a lot and made a lot of progress. That meant they deserved a break.

First, they served the colonel some dinner. He tried

a few bites of Stevie's concoction and then explained that he'd actually had something to eat at the base. The girls weren't convinced that was actually true, but it seemed a very polite way to turn down the coagulated, reheated mass of soup and spaghetti they'd eaten, so they didn't fuss. They did notice, however, that he seemed to eat a lot of popcorn, so at least his stomach was getting filled.

The popcorn had been prepared to go with the movie that they all watched together. Since the girls were horse crazy and Colonel Hanson was crazy about old movies, it made a lot of sense that their choice for the night was *The Treasure of the Sierra Madre*. It had horses, good guys, bad guys, and Humphrey Bogart. Everybody enjoyed it thoroughly.

5

Lisa got to Pine Hollow early on Monday. She dashed over there straight from school without bothering to go home first and change her clothes. She was meeting May so they could work together on their project, but before she did that, she wanted to look in on the mare.

Lisa had learned a lot about mares and foaling since she'd started riding. She'd read some things; they'd talked about others at Horse Wise; she'd overheard Judy, the vet, discussing it with Max; and she and her friends had even assisted at the birth of the stable's own colt, Samson. One of the things she knew about foaling was that mares seemed to have a tendency to want to be alone when they delivered their foals. Horse people joked about staying with a mare practically every second and then if they had to go away for a few minutes, to make a phone call or get a cup of coffee, they'd return to the sight of a newborn foal struggling to his or her feet.

Lisa was half convinced that would be the case with this mare. She was more than a little disappointed to see the mare, still very large and obviously still carrying the foal inside her. Judy was there, checking her out when Lisa arrived.

"How's she doing?" Lisa asked.

"Oh, she's fine," Judy said, patting the mare affectionately on her neck. "Just fine." Judy stood up and put her stethoscope back into her bag. "Everything's right on schedule."

"She'll be delivering soon, won't she?" Lisa asked.

"Ten days, two weeks," Judy said. "That's the way I figure it."

Lisa recalled that she'd been irritated when her friends hadn't asked Judy her question. This was her chance to ask Judy herself.

"Yesterday the mare was acting a little strange. She was kind of edgy. Isn't that a sign that she's about to foal?"

"It can be," Judy said. Lisa was pleased to hear that.

42

"Often mares do get edgy right before their labor begins. I don't think that's the case here, though. I could be wrong, but this lady has another week or two to go."

Lisa heard what Judy said, but she just had a strong feeling she knew better. On the other hand, it was becoming very clear that nobody was going to believe her and the only way for her to be proved correct was for the mare to foal soon. That would happen within a day or two and then everybody would know that Lisa had been right. Lisa smiled, thinking about how wonderful it would be. It was going to be a two-part wonderful. First, it would be wonderful to see a foal. Newborns were so cute! Second, it was going to be wonderful to have been right. Lisa relished the thought of saying "I told you so."

Judy closed up her instrument case and gave the mare a final pat. "See you tomorrow," she told the horse. "You, too," she said to Lisa.

Lisa waved good-bye as the vet walked off. There was something very right about the fact that the vet would say good-bye to the horse before she said it to the person standing there. Lisa gave the mare a pat as well and then went in search of May.

She found May in the tack room, studying the harness for the pony cart.

"Where's the book?" May asked, looking at Lisa's empty hands. That was when Lisa realized that she'd forgotten to bring the paperback Max had given her. Not only had she forgotten to bring it but she'd also forgotten to look at it.

"I left it at Carole's," Lisa answered truthfully. "I'm sorry."

"It doesn't matter," May said. "My mother took me to the tack shop yesterday so I could look at the different kinds of harnesses and they had a copy of the book. I bought it for myself. Isn't it a great book? I spent most of last night looking at it. It's really good, but I did have some questions. I bet it was all clear to you, though, wasn't it?"

Lisa had an uncomfortable feeling. She'd been a straight-A student from her first day at school and she wasn't accustomed to not knowing the answer to questions—especially ones she ought to know. She suspected there were a lot of things she ought to know by now about harnesses. She didn't want to admit her ignorance—or her carelessness.

"Mostly, it was clear to me," Lisa said. "And if you try to explain to me everything you learned about harnesses, I'm sure it will all become clear to you, too."

That sounded just like something one of Lisa's

44

teachers might have said to her when they wanted her to work harder. She hoped May wouldn't realize that it also meant Lisa didn't know what she was doing.

"Okay," May agreed readily. "Well, first of all, this whole thing together is called the harness. And it has a lot of parts. I don't think I can remember all the names. . . ."

"That's okay," Lisa said, trying to sound encouraging. "The most important part is knowing what each of the parts does."

May looked puzzled. "I thought we were just supposed to know how to put it on, not how it works."

"Well, that, too," Lisa said quickly. "Do you know how to put it on?"

May studied the mass of leather that hung on the wall of the tack room. "I did read a lot about it," she said. Her fingers sorted through the leather straps as she considered the situation. "The book made it sound pretty easy. I don't think it's all that easy, but I might be able to do it if you help me." She reached to remove the harness from its hook.

"Sure I'll help," said Lisa.

"Not too much, though," May insisted. "I'd like to be able to do it by myself."

"I promise," Lisa said. "Not too much." She was

genuinely relieved. "Tell you what. I'll start by getting Nickel out of his stall."

"Okay," May agreed.

Lisa hurried to Nickel's stall. She had absolutely no idea what to do with any of the parts of the pony's harness. Not only did she not know what they were called, but she didn't know where they went or even how they went. She hoped May remembered what she'd learned from the book.

A few minutes later, she found that May had learned a lot and remembered it well.

"First comes the collar," May said, approaching Nickel confidently. She slid the circle of leather over the pony's head. May lived on a farm outside of Willow Creek and had been around horses since she was born. She was confident and knowledgeable and she had obviously studied hard.

"You have to be careful of these things, though— traces, I think. That's what they are called, aren't they?"

"Hmm?"

"These long things—they are the traces?" May repeated. She was pointing to a set of long straps that extended from the collar.

"Those are reins, aren't they?" Lisa asked.

"Very clever!" said May, completely missing the

fact that Lisa had no idea what she was talking about. "But you can't fool me with that. Nope, these are the traces, definitely. The reins have to extend from the bit, not the collar. I bet Max tried that very same question on you and you got it right, too, didn't you?"

"Uh, sure," Lisa said.

May continued working on the harness and Lisa was pleased to see that the little girl really did know what she was doing. She'd read hard, studied hard, and learned. Max's idea of a Big Sis/Little Sis project was working, though perhaps not exactly the way Max had had in mind. Still, since the main purpose was for the Little Sis to learn how to do something, it *was* working. There were times when just the presence of an older and wiser person was enough inspiration for a younger student. This appeared to be one of them. Lisa's job, then, became to hold the pony still while May did the work. Lisa was mesmerized by the tangle of leather and buckles and rings and watched in fascination while May methodically untangled them and put them where they belonged, talking all the while, and explaining what she was doing.

"And then here comes the saddle pad—isn't it funny that it's called that even though it really isn't a saddle at all, just this beltlike thing?"

"Uh-huh," Lisa mumbled. She'd been patting Nickel and not paying too much attention.

"Anyway, we don't fasten the saddle pad until after we've got the tail through this thing—I don't remember what it's called. What is it?"

Lisa looked up. There was a leather strap with a loop at the end that apparently reached from the saddle pad to the horse's tail. She had no idea what it was called and wasn't sure how to answer May. Then she had a thought.

"Don't worry about names," she assured May. "It's much more important to know what it does than to know what it's called."

"So what does it do?" May asked.

"It holds the horse's tail in place," Lisa said. Then she groaned to herself, realizing what a dumb thing that was to say. A horse's tail was not actually likely to move very far from the horse's rear.

May didn't think it had been a stupid thing to say. She thought Lisa was just being funny. She laughed.

Lisa's mind was not on the task at hand. It was on the mare; it was on the Know-Down; it was everyplace but on the pony and his harness. Lisa knew that she ought to be paying more attention to what May had learned and what she was doing, but May seemed to be doing just fine without any help from her. Be-

48

sides, she had another five days before the next Horse Wise meeting and in that time Lisa would certainly be able to learn a thing or two about harnesses—enough to help May, as if she needed any help at all. May had learned everything in two days; Lisa could surely learn something in five.

"Wait a minute here," May said. A frown had crossed her face. "I think this is supposed to go that way—" She held up a long piece of leather. "And that one"—she pointed to another piece of leather, drooping on the floor of the stable—"ought to go over here, because it's got to reach to the—oh, no. I should have done this one first."

With that, she began unbuckling and retrying. She flipped the straps across, tangling and untangling them. She couldn't get it right. Finally, she turned to Lisa.

"I haven't done this right at all, have I?" she asked.

Lisa wasn't sure how to answer that. Clearly May had done a lot of it right, but then she'd gotten some of the longer leathers confused. The problem was that Lisa couldn't help her straighten them out. "Looks like you need to do a little bit more studying," she said finally.

"I guess so." May was resigned. "I thought I could do it. I really did. Do you still want to work with me?"

"Of course," said Lisa. "In fact, I'm impressed. You did the whole front of the harness correctly. It has to be correct. Look how well everything fits, but something is definitely wrong back here." She pointed to the rear of the horse where the straps and buckles were still all in a confused mess.

"I'd better go study some more," said May. "Can I try again tomorrow? Then if I don't do it right, you can show me how, but I'd like to be able to do it on my own."

"You will, I'm sure," Lisa said. And she meant it. May was so determined that she probably would have everything figured out by tomorrow.

Lisa helped May remove the rig from Nickel and then took the pony back to his stall while May hung the harness back up in the tack room.

While Lisa was walking the pony through the stable, she began to have a twinge of a feeling that she should have been the one to hang up the harness— she might have learned something about it. But when Lisa passed the mare's stall on the way back from depositing Nickel in his stall, all thoughts of the Big Sister project fled her mind. The mare was acting fidgety again.

Lisa reached up to pat the horse, trying to calm her.

50

She held the mare's halter and stroked her cheek. The mare seemed to like that.

"It's okay, girl," Lisa whispered into the horse's silky ear. "You and I know what's going on, even if nobody else does. I'll be back here tomorrow and you can show off your newborn baby, okay?"

The mare seemed to relax a little. Her ears perked up, her tail flicked gently. Lisa was glad she'd been able to help. She gave the mare a final pat and returned to the tack room to find May.

CAROLE ALWAYS ENJOYED her quiet moments in the stable with Starlight. He was a wonderful horse, beautiful, gentle, loyal. Best of all, he was hers.

When she'd finished working in his stall, grooming, feeding, and watering him, she gave him a final hug. She could have sworn he hugged her back. She laughed to herself at the soft tickle of his chin on her neck. Finally she slid his stall door closed behind her and latched it.

"See you later," she said, bidding Starlight farewell. He snorted in return. She then headed for the tack room where she was pretty sure she'd find Stevie and Lisa waiting for her. The three of them had made plans on the phone the night before to meet at Pine Hollow to do some more drill work for the Know-Down.

Stevie was in the tack room, but Lisa wasn't. May Grover was also there. The little girl appeared to be completely wrapped in the long leathers of the cart harness. Stevie was trying to untangle her from them, but it wasn't working very well.

"That's not the martingale, that's the loin strap," May was saying. "The martingale is this one and if you untie the knot it's in, I think I can do the rest myself."

Stevie tugged at the leather as she'd been told. In a minute, May emerged, holding the harness neatly.

"There," she said, victoriously.

"Nice work," Stevie said.

"You helped me."

"I didn't mean that. Anybody could have untangled them. The nice part was knowing the difference between the martingale and the loin strap. You've been working with Lisa on that stuff, haven't you?"

"I sure have and she's a great teacher," said May. "She knows exactly how to get me to work hard and learn a lot. Yesterday I couldn't finish hitching up Nickel and instead of just doing it for me, she made me learn to do it by myself. Today I'm sure I'm going

53

to do it. I spent a lot of time reading about it last night. Now, can you hold the door open so I can carry this thing over to Nickel's stall?"

"Certainly." Stevie obliged. May had nearly wrapped herself in the harness to keep it from tangling any more. She walked out of the tack room like a queen with a royal train made of leather. Stevie and Carole loved watching her. She reminded them of themselves when they were younger—so eager to learn everything there was to know about horses.

Just as May was leaving the tack room, Lisa arrived. Lisa offered to carry one end of the harness, but May assured her she could do it by herself.

"I want to try to do this all alone," May said. "Please?"

"Okay," Lisa agreed, rather too quickly as far as Carole was concerned. Carole knew enough about harnessing a horse to know it was a two-person job, but she didn't want to interfere with the Big Sis/Little Sis project. So far, it appeared to be working all right if she could judge by how much May seemed to have learned. Lisa seemed to know what she was doing as a teacher, judging by what May had already learned. She no doubt had her reasons now. Carole kept her concerns to herself.

"Where were you?" Stevie asked Lisa.

"I was checking on the mare. She still hasn't foaled."

"I know," Carole said. "Judy says she's got a couple of weeks to go."

Lisa shrugged.

Stevie thought Lisa looked annoyed, but there were too many other things happening to ask her what was going on.

"We've got to work on the study sheets some more," Stevie said. "Where can we go?"

"I've got an idea," Carole said. "Prancer's box stall is empty while she's at the trainer's this week. We can sit in there in the fresh straw. There's a class going on, so we should have some privacy."

"Good idea," Stevie agreed. "I want to keep our study techniques to ourselves. We don't want to give anything to the enemy, do we?"

Lisa grinned. "Come on, Stevie. The other students are hardly 'the enemy.' But I wouldn't mind beating them."

Carole always liked being in box stalls. It was so horsey. It made her feel even closer to horses than usual. As they settled into the straw in Prancer's stall she decided her friends might think her odd if she told them exactly how she felt, so she didn't. It would be her secret.

Carole pulled a folded bundle of papers from her rear pocket. "Okay, where were we?" She scanned the sheets. "I've got it. What is a cob?"

"Something you eat corn off of?" Stevie offered. Her friends knew she was teasing. She knew the answer to that question as well as Lisa did, but Lisa gave it.

"It's sort of a mix between a horse and a pony," she said. "It's no taller than fifteen point one hands. Its head and neck look like a pony's, but its body and limbs look like those of a horse."

"Two points," Carole said. "What are the four basic kinds of jumps?"

Stevie took that one. "Staircase or ascending oxer, pyramid, upright, and square oxer."

Carole awarded her four points.

"Here's another hard one. Name the parts of the mouth and the head on which the bit and bridle act."

There was silence. Neither Lisa nor Stevie could answer that one. Carole told them. "There are seven parts, and they are: the lips and corners of the mouth, the bars of the mouth, the tongue, the roof of the mouth, the poll, the chin groove, and, last but not least, the nose."

A head appeared over the wall of the neighboring stall. The stall belonged to Garnet. The head was Veronica diAngelo's. The three girls groaned inwardly, but were too polite to do it out loud.

"What are you up to?" Veronica asked.

"We're studying," Stevie said.

"What for?"

"The Know-Down, of course," Stevie said. "Haven't you been studying?" she asked. "Or is that one of those things you get your butler to do for you?"

Veronica gave her a dirty look.

"Certainly I've been studying," she said. "Very hard, in fact. Go ahead, test me."

For a minute Carole was tempted. This was a wonderful opportunity to make life difficult for Veronica. She could find the trickiest question of the bunch and use it on her. But Carole had a strong sense of right and wrong and she knew better than that. She just took the next question on the sheet.

"What's another word for forging?"

Veronica's eyebrows crinkled together in thought. "Isn't that when a horse just eats what it comes across in the wild?"

Carole stifled a snicker. Veronica was confusing *foraging* with *forging*, which was another word for over-reaching. This happened when the horse's hind toe hit the front heel. It meant that the horse's rear stride was too long and required special training to overcome. Carole read the answer from the sheet to Veronica.

"That's in there?" Veronica asked, looking quizzically at the sheaf of papers in Carole's hand.

"Uh-huh," Stevie answered. "As your butler no doubt knows."

This time Stevie couldn't contain her laugh. It was easy to hate Veronica, but it wasn't often that the girls found she actually didn't know something about horses. She was a pretty good horsewoman, except when it came to work she considered dirty or beneath her.

Stevie was working on a couple of follow-up remarks for Veronica. She had in mind something about a remedial riding course, or maybe suggesting that Veronica write the answers to all the questions on the palm of her hand, if she could spell them. Stevie's snide remarks were cut off before they began. There was a shriek from the far side of the stable and the voice was unmistakably May Grover's. The younger girl was in trouble.

In an instant Stevie, Lisa, and Carole dropped everything they were doing, were on their feet and out of the stall, quickly pulling the door closed behind them.

What they found when they got there was May

standing all alone by the open door of the stable with tears streaming down her face. There was no sign of Nickel. There was, however, a cart harness strewn all over the floor.

"He just ran away!" May wailed.

It took only a few seconds to see what had happened. May had opened the door for light and the pony had found the call of the wild just too tempting. When May had unclipped his lead rope, he'd taken off, leaving her alone and miserable.

It wasn't the first time a horse had gotten loose at Pine Hollow, nor would it be the last. The girls knew just what to do. Lisa told May to bring the lead rope and the four of them followed the pony out into the paddock. None of the paddocks that surrounded the stable at Pine Hollow was very large. They were intended for light exercise, not for living quarters. It wouldn't be hard to corner the pony and clip the rope onto his halter as long as he was penned in the paddock.

Unfortunately, he wasn't penned in the paddock. Somebody had left a gate open and Nickel had gone right through it. As they watched, he frolicked in the very large field beyond the paddock. Capturing him had suddenly changed from a two-minute project to a big deal. The girls thought they knew who was responsible for the open gate. There was only one person at Pine Hollow who thought she was too good to close gates behind her and that was Veronica diAngelo.

"I'll go get Starlight," Carole said. "And while I'm in there, I'm going to give Veronica a piece of my mind."

She stormed back into the stable. Starlight's stall was near Garnet's, which was near the empty stall they'd been sitting in. Carole found Garnet alone in her stall. She also found the door to the empty stall open. There was no sign of Veronica. Carole decided she didn't have time to track Veronica down and give her a piece of her mind. It had never worked before. She doubted if it would do any good this time. Also, she just wanted to get Nickel back where he belonged and for that she'd need Starlight's help. She slid the empty stall door closed again and then turned to fetch Starlight.

Secretly Carole was a little happy at the opportunity that had arisen for her. Most of the time when she rode Starlight, it was in class or on a training course. This was the real thing—using a horse for work. And, since she was in such a hurry, she wasn't going to use a saddle. She'd just hop on his bare back, no bridle, just his halter with a lead rope attached, and they'd ride the way she imagined people were intended to ride horses: horse and rider, nothing else.

As quickly as she could, she led him back to the door from which Nickel had escaped. Then, once out of the stable, Carole hiked herself up onto his warm silken back, and taking the lead rope from May's hands, she and Starlight rode off after the runaway pony.

It took a while. Nickel seemed to like the idea of his freedom. He also sensed that the bareback rider carrying a lead rope didn't like the idea of Nickel's freedom. He took off.

Carole watched Nickel dodge to her left. With her right leg, she moved Starlight over the same way. He responded instantly, as if he understood the task and it was a good thing he did, too, because Nickel was prepared to make this as difficult as possible. Every time Nickel moved to one side, Starlight followed, only to find that Nickel had already changed his mind —and his direction. He was a very clever pony. Carole was a clever girl, though, and Starlight was Nickel's match.

Carole and Starlight managed to herd Nickel toward a corner of the field. Stevie, Lisa, and May ran over to where they were. It took all four girls and one very clever horse to corner the pony. It also took almost an hour. Finally, and triumphantly, Carole clipped the lead rope onto the pony's halter.

She handed the end of the rope to Lisa. She wasn't sure how resentful the pony might be and didn't think it safe for May to hold him. However, the pony was well-trained and the minute Lisa tugged on the lead rope, Nickel behaved just the way he was supposed to. He was docile and obedient. Lisa gave the lead rope to May. The pony followed and didn't give her any trouble at all.

"Well, there goes an hour of study time," Lisa said glumly.

"It's okay," Stevie said. "We had fun."

"Sure, but we did lose the time and I've got to get home."

"Me, too," Carole agreed. "Dad's picking me up at the shopping center because he's going to the supermarket."

"Maybe we can walk over there together and test ourselves as we go," Lisa suggested. As a straight-A student, she'd devised a lot of ways to find study time when there wasn't any study time to be had.

"Okay by me," Stevie agreed. "You've got the sheets, Carole?"

Carole patted her back pocket, expecting to find

the familiar bulge of the papers there. But this time her pocket was empty.

"I must have left them in the empty stall," she said. She recalled jumping up to go to May's rescue. She didn't recall putting the pages back in her pocket. Nor did she recall seeing them when she went to get Starlight.

As soon as they reached the stable, Carole dismounted and walked Starlight back to his stall. She patted him as they walked, and told him how wonderful he'd been. He seemed to understand. At least he nodded.

As soon as she'd closed his stall door, she walked over to the empty stall. Oddly, the door was once again open. Carole peered in. There, on the floor, in a corner where she hadn't been sitting, she saw the sheets for the Know-Down. She didn't know how they'd gotten there—she must have thrown them there herself as she ran to help May. It didn't matter, though. She had them.

She met her friends at the front door of Pine Hollow. "What's the difference between a body clip and a trace clip?" Carole asked.

"I know, I know," Lisa said eagerly.

They were back in the groove.

Two steps outside of Pine Hollow, the girls stopped. May was standing by the driveway, her head hanging down. She seemed very upset about something and oblivious to her surroundings.

"What's up, May?" Stevie asked.

It took a while for the young girl to answer. She looked as though she was trying to get up the courage to answer what Stevie had thought was a pretty easy question.

"I'm just so ashamed," May answered finally.

"Of what?" Lisa asked.

Carole didn't need to ask, though. She understood. "It wasn't your fault," she said. "Really."

"But he shouldn't have run away!"

Then Lisa and Stevie understood, too. May thought that everything that had happened with Nickel was her own fault and that just wasn't the case.

May looked at Lisa for a confirmation.

"It really wasn't your fault," Lisa said. "It happened because Veronica left the gate open. If there's one lesson that Max teaches us again and again, it's that we always have to close gates that we've opened. Veronica learned that the very first day she ever rode at Pine Hollow—"

"—and forgot it that same day," Stevie said, finishing Lisa's sentence for her.

May snuffled and then laughed. "I shouldn't have let go of Nickel, though, should I?" she asked.

"No, but everybody makes mistakes," Carole said. Then, glancing at Lisa, she continued, "Even us, sometimes."

Lisa didn't notice Carole's look, but she was aware of May's unhappiness. She wanted to reassure the young girl some more.

"Don't worry about it," Lisa said. "Maybe it was a mistake, but, like Carole said, lots of people make mistakes and that's why you've got friends—to help you out when you need it. We were there, we helped you out. No problem. And we'd be glad to help you out again, but I bet you won't make that same mistake again, will you?"

"No way," May promised. "I really learned something today."

"Good, because learning is what riding is all about," Lisa said. She smiled. Lisa was pleased with all the progress that May was making and was glad to know that she had at least a small part in it. May was such a smart girl and so eager that it was a pleasure to work with her on anything.

"There's something else I'd like to know about, too," May said.

"Ask away," Carole offered. Carole was never happier than when she had a chance to explain something about horses. Often her explanations were a good deal longer than the questions, but that didn't stop her from sharing them.

May reached into her backpack and pulled out a bunch of papers. "It's this study sheet Max gave us," she said. "Can you help me with it?"

"No problem," Stevie assured her. "And it's not surprising that you're finding it a challenge. We are, too. Ask away!"

May squinted in the fading light of the day and scanned the papers, flipping them as she looked for something. "Oh, yeah, here it is. Under the 'Call the

Vet' section, it says 'Below normal temperature.' I thought only a fever was a bad sign, how could a low temperature be a bad sign?"

Carole took the question. "You have to understand what a fever actually indicates," she began. "An animal's normal body temperature rises when the animal's defense system kicks in, getting warmed up to fight an infection, any kind of infection. Actually, this is true of humans, too. Anyway, in a sense, a fever is a good sign because it means the horse's body is doing what it's supposed to do. When the temperature is below normal and the animal is sick, it can mean that the animal's own immune system has given up. That means the animal is *very* sick."

"Oh," May said, thinking about the information Carole had given her. "It makes sense now. Thanks. I just couldn't understand what the study sheet meant. You've made it much clearer. I mean, look at what Max wrote here." She pointed to the study sheet. "It was so confusing—" May handed the papers to Carole.

Carole was indeed confused, but not in the way May thought she was. She glanced at the pages she now held and then she looked more carefully. They didn't look anything at all like the sheets from which she, Lisa, and Stevie had been studying. They included lists of information, not questions and answers. They weren't divided by point value, either. They had some of the same information and then a lot more.

"Let me see," Stevie said, taking the papers from Carole's hands. Lisa tried to look over Stevie's shoulder but was interrupted when a car pulled up in front of them. The driver's window rolled down. Mrs. Grover waved at her daughter.

"May, dear! Time to go home!"

May retrieved her papers from Stevie's hands, once again thanked the Saddle Club girls for all their help, and climbed into the car to drive home. She waved as her mother drove off.

"What was that?" Stevie asked, confused.

"Mrs. Grover," Lisa replied, somewhat surprised that Stevie apparently didn't recognize the woman.

"No, not her. The papers. What were they?"

"The study sheets," Lisa said. Why was Stevie being so flaky about May and Mrs. Grover?

"You didn't see them, did you?" Carole asked her.

"I've spent hours looking at those study sheets," Lisa said.

"Not those," said Carole.

"What are you two talking about?" asked Lisa.

"I wish I knew," Stevie said.

"I think I do," Carole said. "And I don't think I

like it at all. You're not going to like it, either. This calls for an emergency meeting of The Saddle Club. Right now. Right here."

Lisa and Stevie knew when Carole was serious and she clearly was serious about this. Carole told her friends to go to the feed room, that she'd meet them there in a few minutes. The three of them returned to the stable. Lisa and Stevie headed for the feed room while Carole dashed off on a mysterious errand.

"What is this all about?" Lisa asked.

"I'm not sure what it is, but I am sure we're not going to like it," Stevie said. That was a very Stevie-like answer, but it didn't satisfy Lisa's curiosity. It did, however, tell her all she was going to learn until Carole returned.

"Here," Carole said, entering the feed room. She was carrying three sets of papers—one for each of them. Lisa and Stevie looked at them. At first glance, it appeared to be the question-and-answer sheet the three of them had been studying from since Saturday. At second glance it was a very different set of papers, indeed.

"What is this?" Lisa asked, but she was beginning to get the feeling that she already knew the answer to the question.

"This is the set of sheets Max gave us on Saturday."

"But it's not what we've been studying from," Stevie said. "How did that happen?"

"We've been studying from the sheets you took from Dad's desk," Carole said.

Then Stevie understood. "Oh no. He's a parent volunteer at Horse Wise and Max gave all the parent volunteers the actual questions and answers he's planning to use at the Know-Down. He must want them to be familiar with the questions he'd be asking and the correct answers, right?"

"Right," Carole said.

Lisa put a hand over her mouth. "That's why your dad said he didn't want you snooping on his desk."

"I thought it had to do with my birthday, but it wasn't that at all," said Carole.

"I should have known," said Stevie.

"Why?"

"Well, first of all because your birthday is a couple of months off yet. And second of all, there wasn't anything in the least bit personal on his desk. I mean, if there had been anything to snoop, you know I would have snooped it."

"I know," Carole said. "That's why I assumed you were lying when you told me that you hadn't seen anything interesting. You wouldn't have told me anyway."

"Oh, I don't know," Stevie said. "You know I'm no good with a secret."

It was true, but Carole and Lisa didn't bother to respond. They had something else on their minds.

There was a long silence. The grain room was a good place for silence because it was filled with barrels of grain and a small stack of hay bales. The effect was to baffle all sounds and make it like a soundproof room—a good place for a private discussion.

"You know what this means, don't you?" Stevie asked after a while.

"It means we're cheating," said Lisa, who had never considered cheating on anything in her entire life.

"That wasn't what I had in mind," said Stevie, who *had* considered cheating many times, but had always rejected it. "What it means is that we're just about guaranteed to do better on the Know-Down than anybody else."

"True," said Carole. "We've been working very hard, too, and I know we're learning a lot."

"We're learning the things we're supposed to learn," said Lisa, who was beginning to think like Stevie. "Also, I know from experience in taking tests —and doing pretty well on them—that the teachers usually focus on the most important information when they give a test. All the things they ask questions about are the things they really want you to know. The point is that Max must have put the very most important information into the questions he intends to ask. That's what we *ought* to be focusing on. And since we've been studying exactly that, it *is* what we've been focusing on. We're learning what he wants us to learn."

"And we're learning it so well that we'll do better than anybody else," Stevie repeated. Her eyes were gleaming.

Carole was thinking about Cam. When they'd first found out about the Know-Down, Carole and Stevie had decided that it didn't matter whether the boys beat them. But now that the event was drawing closer, Carole realized that she did care about doing well. In fact she really wanted to win.

She flipped through the study sheets she'd just gotten from Mrs. Reg again. They were packed with detailed information about riding, horse care, stable management, horse health, training. There was a *lot* more on the study sheets than on the question-and-answer sheets, but it wasn't as if The Saddle Club hadn't been working. "Lisa's right, you know," Carole said finally.

That was what sealed it for Lisa and Stevie. Before Carole had spoken, they'd each had some doubts about what they were doing. When it came to fun, Stevie was their leader. If the issue had to do with logical thinking, they turned to Lisa. But in the matters of horse care, Carole was definitely ahead of her friends and they respected everything she had to say on the subject. If Carole thought that studying from the question-and-answer sheet was all right because it was the most important information, that was good enough for them.

"Max would be furious if he found out," said Stevie. Since she was the acknowledged expert at adults getting annoyed, her friends had to agree.

"And besides," Lisa said, suddenly finding a third compelling reason for them to keep their advantage to themselves. "Think of all the work that's involved."

"How's that?" Stevie asked.

"It must have taken Max an awfully long time to put this together," Lisa said. "If we tell him what happened, not only will he be angry but he'll also have to make up a whole new set of questions and answers. That's hard work!"

"And they won't include the most important information," said Carole.

It was decided, then. The girls had considered every single aspect of the whole situation and had come to the logical conclusion. They hadn't meant to get the actual questions and answers for the Know-Down, but it had happened by mistake. Trying to rectify that mistake would just cause a lot of people, especially Max, a lot of trouble. And since the purpose of the Know-Down was to make them learn the important things and they *were* learning the important things, the whole world would be better off if they kept their secret to themselves.

Carole glanced at her watch. "Yikes. My dad's waiting for me at the grocery store. I've got to go."

"So we're all in agreement?" Stevie asked.

Lisa and Carole solemnly nodded. Then the three of them shook hands and left the stable.

"STEVIE, IT'S FOR you," her brother Chad grumbled. The grumble from her older brother meant two things. First, it meant Chad was disappointed the phone call wasn't for him. Second, it meant it was Stevie's friend, Phil. When Chad's girlfriend *didn't* call but Stevie's boyfriend *did,* Chad tended to grumble in a particularly obnoxious way.

"Hi," Stevie said cheerfully into the phone. Chad's grumbles always made her particularly cheerful.

"How can you be so happy?" Phil began. "From the moment I opened the envelope you sent me with the study sheets, I've been tearing my hair out. I can't believe how much material your Max wants us to learn in ten days!"

Stevie's first inclination was to gloat. Instead she tried to be encouraging. "Oh, don't worry about it, Phil," she said. "You already know about half of that stuff, maybe more. If you get half the questions right, you'll be doing pretty well. And, then whatever you learn from the sheets between now and then will make you do better."

"Half?" he responded. "Is that all you expect? I'll have you know that when the Cross County Pony Club had a Know-Down last year, my team got the highest overall score."

That was the sort of information that usually made Stevie cringe. But this time she had an advantage he'd never know about.

"I'm sure you'll get more than half the questions, Phil," Stevie assured him. "In fact, I'm pretty sure you'll do very well. I have to warn you, though, Lisa and Carole and I have been studying like mad. So, though you'll do well, you shouldn't expect to do as well as we will."

Phil knew a challenge when he heard one. "You think so? You think that just because you invited me, I won't try to beat you?"

"Not for a minute," Stevie said. "It's just that I

have the funny feeling that no matter how hard you try, you won't be able to beat me."

Now she was gloating and she knew it. It wasn't her favorite part of her own character, but when Phil egged her on like that—well, she couldn't help herself.

"I saw a newborn foal today," Phil said. It was a pretty smooth change of subject. Phil and Stevie were both aware of their tendency to be competitive. There was a sort of unwritten rule between them that when they started trying to top one another, somebody better change the subject.

"Oh, cute?"

"Very," Phil said. "He was just a couple of days old."

"We're going to have a new foal at Pine Hollow soon," Stevie said. Then she explained about Geronimo and how the mare he would mate was almost ready to foal. "Judy says it's going to be a week or ten days. The foal might even be born by the time you come for the Know-Down."

"That would be nice. There's something so special about the little ones."

"I love their long, spindly legs," Stevie said. "They hardly look strong enough to hold the animal up."

The two of them continued talking for a while.

There seemed to be so much to talk about. They talked about foals, then riding, then when they seemed to be approaching the issue of the Know-Down again, they switched to school. When Chad stuck his head into Stevie's room for a third time to scowl—indicating he was almost certain his girlfriend was desperately trying to call him—Stevie thought maybe she ought to say good-night to Phil.

"See you next week," she said.

"Bye," he said.

Stevie cradled the phone and then bounded up off her bed. She went in search of Chad so she could yell at him for interrupting her very private phone call. She would have done it, too, except that the phone rang again and it was for Chad—the call he'd been waiting for.

She went to work on her homework instead.

CAROLE'S FATHER SWIRLED the ground meat around in the frying pan. "You've got to break it up just so and brown it perfectly, otherwise your chili won't be as good as mine."

Carole listened attentively. She'd been given the job of chopping an onion for him and she found that if she ignored how much the onion was making her eyes water, they seemed to water less.

"You're a wonderful teacher," she said, encouraging him to keep on talking.

"I don't know about that," said Colonel Hanson. "You listen most of the time when I talk, but there's a certain lieutenant in my office who appears to have a serious hearing difficulty."

The frown on his face told Carole he was genuinely worried about something. She asked him what it was.

"Oh, it was that problem the other night. It never should have happened, you know, but this lieutenant was listening to something he shouldn't have been listening to and overheard a private conversation."

"You mean like on purpose?" she asked.

"Not really. Maybe if he had been listening intentionally, he would have gotten it right and would have kept his mouth closed. As it was, he heard it wrong and he told some people about it. It got a whole lot of people very upset."

"Did this have something to do with national security?" Carole asked. Since Colonel Hanson was in the Marine Corps there was that potential, but her father assured her it wasn't.

"No, our borders are safe," he teased. "But the lieutenant's carelessness caused a lot of trouble. I've been smoothing ruffled feathers since Saturday. Oh, there it is!" The triumphant tone was unmistakable and didn't seem to Carole to have anything to do with the lieutenant. It turned out that she was right. He was talking about the chili. "See, when the meat begins bubbling just like that, then it's really cooking and should start browning properly. Are you going to grate the cheese, too? That won't make you cry the way the onions do."

"Uh, sure," she said, scooping the onions into a bowl. She took the jack cheese out of the refrigerator and unhooked the cheese grater from the pegboard. "So tell me more about the lieutenant," she said.

Her father shook his head in distress. "Oh, I don't know," he said. "I could tell you more, but it just upsets me so. The man had no business doing what he was doing and even less talking about it. He's a grown-up and should understand that private means private!"

With that, he gave the meat an extra stir and splattered some of it onto the range. The flame sizzled and spat. Carole took a cloth and wiped it up. Her father's words echoed in her ear as she worked. *If only he knew*, she thought.

She remembered him telling her and her friends to stay away from his desk. She remembered telling Stevie it would be okay because it had to do with her birthday. She remembered not believing Stevie when she told her there weren't any secrets on the desk. She remembered not thinking there was anything wrong with what they'd done. But then she'd found out that there was something wrong with what they'd done. It didn't make her feel good. In fact, it made her feel pretty rotten.

She wanted to tell. She was bursting to tell. She couldn't stand keeping a secret from her wonderful, trusting father. But if she told him, what would he say? He'd be as angry with her as he was with the lieutenant. There wasn't any difference between what they'd done, except that the lieutenant had told other people. Carole hadn't done that. She and her friends would keep the secret forever.

A secret from her father, forever? The very thought was overwhelming to Carole. How could she not tell her father something important like that? She felt a swelling rise up in her throat. Tears welled in her eyes.

Her father looked at her, alarmed.

"It's the onions," she said, wiping away a tear that rolled down her cheek.

LISA LOOKED HARD at the page, as if staring could make the words more sensible—or memorable. Then she closed the book and looked up at the ceiling, attempting to recite what she'd just been attempting to read.

"First comes the collar, then the saddle pad, and you tighten the girth, then you do the thing that goes around the horse's tail—" She'd already forgotten the word. She looked at the book. She found that she hadn't just forgotten the word. She'd also forgotten what she'd read.

"All right," she said aloud. "It's called the crupper —that's the thing that goes around the tail—and you *don't* do it then. You do it *before* you tighten the girth. Then next comes . . ."

Once again she couldn't remember. She was very frustrated with herself. She usually was good at learning, particularly memorizing and reciting, but this wasn't sinking in at all. The problem was the Know-Down. Actually there were two problems to do with the Know-Down. The first one was that there was an awful lot about the Know-Down that she and her friends still had to work on. Once Lisa and May did their demonstration at Horse Wise, which was scheduled for tomorrow, Lisa would have more time to concentrate on learning. Luckily, Lisa reminded herself, Stevie and Carole have been riding for a long time. They'll see to it that I learn everything I need to know. And, of course, the three of them had an advantage.

Lisa felt a twinge of conscience. That was the second problem with the Know-Down. If the mix-up with the questions had happened at school, it would be wrong. But Pine Hollow wasn't school and the Know-Down wasn't a test. It was a game and the idea was to show how much you had learned and how much you understood. For the past two weeks The Saddle Club had been working hard on accomplishing that very goal.

Lisa dismissed her uncomfortable feelings and looked again at the book about harnesses. The next thing it talked about was breeching. What was that? She studied the chart and couldn't find it at all. It probably didn't matter. May almost certainly knew exactly what breeching was.

9

TUESDAY WASN'T AN official Pony Club day, but since almost all the kids in Horse Wise also took riding class on Tuesday afternoons, Max sometimes used the class time as if it were a meeting. Sometimes it seemed that the main difference was that on Tuesdays he'd start the class by saying "Riders, come to order!" On Saturdays, it was "Horse Wise, come to order!"

Max had arranged it so that after the formal riding class, May and Lisa would do their demonstration and explanation.

While they were tacking up for class, Lisa asked May if she was nervous.

"I don't think so," May said. "We really worked

very hard on this and I'm pretty sure we can do it. Besides, I know that if I goof up on something, you'll be able to help me." May gave a final tug to her horse's girth, checked the stirrup length, and prepared to mount.

Lisa watched the younger girl as she did these things, admiring the way she did them. When Lisa had been May's age, she'd never ridden a horse at all. And now there was May, just about half as old as Lisa was and very good at everything she did with horses. Lisa wondered briefly who was actually the Big Sis and who was the Little Sis in this project. Smiling to herself with the thought, she turned her attention to Barq's girth and the length of the stirrups on his saddle. She wouldn't want her saddle to slip off in the middle of class—especially in front of her Little Sis!

Class was, as usual, quite wonderful, though, as usual, Max made them work very hard. Max was working on gait changes, and at first Lisa thought he was doing it primarily for the newer riders. Changing gaits was something a rider learned in the second or third class. She found, however, that he was being a lot tougher on the more experienced riders than he was on the newer riders.

"You don't have to tell the whole world you want your horse to slow down, just tell your horse," he told them all. Then he explained that a well-trained rider could give all kinds of instructions to his or her horse without making any of it obvious. A small amount of pressure on the reins was as informative to the horse as a big yank, and much less painful. Sitting into the saddle was just as effective as—and much more proper than—a rider straightening his or her legs as if digging heels into the sand.

They tried it again and again. Max had them walk, trot, and then stop. Finally, when he wasn't frowning so much—meaning he thought they were doing pretty well—he let them trot for a while and then canter. Lisa wasn't sure if she liked cantering or trotting better. Barq had a wonderful smooth canter, but his trot was so brisk that sometimes it felt as if he moved more quickly trotting than cantering.

By the end of class, Lisa thought she'd learned a lot and it seemed a little odd because it was all about a subject she already thought she knew a lot about! That was one of the things she liked best about horseback riding. There was *always* something to learn.

She'd been concentrating so hard on everything Max said that she was almost surprised when he excused her and May from class early so they could get ready for their demonstration. *Their* demonstration? Lisa asked silently. It was really *May's* demonstration.

Lisa was just there to hold Nickel so he wouldn't bolt the way he had when Veronica had left the gate open.

Lisa untacked their horses while May brought the harness to the indoor ring where they were doing the demonstration. Then the two girls pulled the pony cart into the ring and brought Nickel in together. Lisa perched on the fence that surrounded the ring so she could hold Nickel's lead rope while May set all the equipment out just the way she wanted it.

"I like it when all the leathers are kind of laid out the way they will be when the harness is on Nickel. That way, I can point to all the parts for the other riders and explain what I'm going to do *before* I do it. Isn't that the way you like to do it?" May asked.

"Sure," Lisa said, although she wasn't completely sure she understood what May was talking about. Nickel was distracting her. He seemed to have developed the idea that there might be something good to eat in her pocket and was nuzzling her affectionately. He was a cute pony that Lisa had always liked. They were sort of giggling together.

"Good luck," Stevie said.

"Thanks, but I don't need any luck here," Lisa said. "May is doing all the work. This has been a breeze!"

"Yeah, but you had to know what to tell her," Stevie said.

"I had to know what book to have her study from," Lisa corrected her. "And she even bought it for herself!"

"Oh, well, I hope she does a good job."

"No sweat. She's got it cold."

Stevie gave Nickel an affectionate pat and sat down on the bench. Carole joined her.

"Something's wrong," Stevie whispered to Carole.

"I know," Carole said. "We've got to talk."

Stevie wasn't sure what Carole thought was wrong, but she was sure it wasn't what she thought was wrong.

"No, I mean about this demonstration thing," Stevie whispered.

"Is May going to goof up?" Carole asked, quite concerned.

"I don't think so. At least I hope not."

Carole got a funny feeling in her stomach. If Stevie wasn't worried about May, she must mean she was worried about Lisa. If Stevie was worried about Lisa, then Carole needed to be worried, too. The problem was she wasn't sure what she should be worried about.

Max walked into the ring and began speaking. "This is the first of what I think of as Big Sis/Little Sis demonstrations, though of course sometimes there will be brothers—bros?" The riders laughed. Lisa realized later that that was the last time she laughed that afternoon.

May began the demonstration. Before she started putting the harness on the pony, she identified all the main parts of the tack, from the blinkers to the crupper. Then, proceeding carefully, she put the collar on, followed by the saddle pad. It was at that point that Nickel changed his mind about standing still. He decided he didn't really want to have Lisa hold his lead rope. He wanted to walk around a little bit. This was going to take more than two people. Stevie took the lead rope so that Lisa could help May. Lisa hopped down off the fence.

"Here, you do the crupper," May suggested.

Lisa looked at the leathers. She had absolutely no idea what to do. She did know that one of the pieces of leather was supposed to end in a loop and that the pony's tail was supposed to go through it, but she couldn't identify which part went where.

Lisa had a sudden and totally unfamiliar feeling: panic. She didn't know any of the parts of the harness. She had no idea what she was supposed to do next or what it was supposed to accomplish. These were all things May knew. May was the student; Lisa was the teacher. May was *supposed* to learn. Teachers didn't learn. They taught. May just hadn't needed any teaching; she'd done it all herself. So Lisa hadn't done any learning.

She stammered, more uncomfortable with the situation than she could ever remember being in her life. She looked at her friends. They looked back at her and the only thing their looks told her was that she was in every bit as much trouble as she thought she was. Her friends knew her best. They would know before anybody else. Maybe nobody else knew yet. Lisa looked at the other students. They were figuring it out.

"Here, Lisa," Stevie said. "Why don't you hold Nickel again. He seems calmer with you. I'll give May a hand. You just let us know if we make any mistakes, okay?"

"Okay," Lisa said numbly. She held Nickel's lead and watched, barely taking in anything that happened.

"Tell me what I have to do, May," Stevie said. And May did. While the class watched, and learned, May explained everything Stevie had to do in order to hitch the pony to the wagon. May talked constantly, naming each piece of the harness, explaining where it would go, how to put it there, and what it would do. Stevie followed her directions to the letter and within ten minutes, Nickel was completely hitched to the wagon. During the entire process, Lisa hardly moved at all. She pasted a smile on her face that nobody believed.

Stevie and May invited her into the cart for a ride. Lisa climbed in back while May and Stevie sat in the driver's seat and drove Lisa around the ring once. It reminded Lisa of the very first time she'd ever touched a pony. She'd been four years old and her parents had let her have a pony-cart ride at a local park. She remembered that, at that time, she hadn't known anything at all about horses and had dreamed of a day when she might know a lot. Lisa wondered now when that day might come.

Once the cart had circled the ring, Max dismissed the class. Carole and Stevie helped Lisa and May, but mostly May, remove the cart and the harness from the pony.

Max came over. Lisa dreaded hearing what he had to say. She had totally failed and she knew it. She'd been under the mistaken impression that the only person who had had anything to learn was May. The fact that May *had* learned was good, but May hadn't learned the way Max had wanted her to learn. Max had wanted Lisa to *teach*. However, a teacher who was unwilling to learn could never teach. Lisa had let May down, she'd let Max down, and worst of all, she'd let herself down. She'd totally blown an opportunity to learn and to help. Max was certainly furious with her and he was right to be. Lisa braced herself for the worst.

To her surprise, Max put his arm around Lisa's shoulder while he spoke to May.

"May, you've done a lot of work," he said. That, at least was true. "I'm really impressed." Then he spoke more slowly. "I think we've all learned a lot from this first attempt at Big Sis/Little Sis projects, haven't we?"

"I sure have," May said. Everyone knew that was true.

"Me, too," Lisa mumbled. That was true, too, but Lisa had done all her learning in the last five minutes. Max gave her shoulders a warm squeeze. Somehow he just knew.

THERE WAS MORE unfinished business and all three girls knew it. Although it was time to leave the stable, go home, do homework, bone up more on the Know-Down material, and sort out what really happened to Lisa, none of the three of them was ready to proceed. There was something else they had to do first.

When their own horses were completely tended to, they gathered at the paddock where Samson, the stable's colt, had been playing. Stevie had her grooming bucket. Although Samson didn't seem particularly in need of a grooming, the girls were particularly in need of something to do while they talked. Carole clipped a lead onto Samson's halter and they began grooming the coal-black colt. He liked the attention. They were glad for the opportunity to talk while they combed and brushed.

"It was awful," Lisa said. "I just completely missed the point."

Her friends didn't say anything. They agreed, they understood. They knew it could have been them.

"The point wasn't to be sure May knew all that stuff. The point was for both of us to learn—to learn together. May won't always be there when I want to hitch up a pony to a wagon. And Stevie won't always be there to make me look good. I can pretend to Max, maybe even to you two. . . ." She looked at her friends. "All right, not to you two, but anyway, I can pretend to other people. Who I can't pretend to is the horse. I mean Nickel isn't exactly able to tell me how to do it, is he?"

"No," Carole answered. "And that's the core of it, isn't it?"

Both Stevie and Lisa knew that Carole wasn't just talking about Lisa then. She was talking about the three of them. She was talking about the Know-Down. "You're not the only one who learned something this afternoon, Lisa," Carole continued.

"We're going to have to tell about the study sheets, aren't we?" Stevie asked.

Carole nodded. So did Lisa.

"I kept trying to figure it out so we wouldn't have to do it. I kept thinking how much fun it would be to score perfectly while Phil was there. I almost had myself convinced."

"What made you see it the other way?" Lisa asked.

"It was thinking about the horses—really what you just said. Nickel couldn't tell you what to do. We can learn everything Max puts on the Know-Down, but what do we do when something comes up that wasn't on the Know-Down question sheets?

"The horses have to come first," Carole said, summing up all of their arguments.

Lisa pulled a comb through Samson's tangled mane and spoke thoughtfully. "You know, I used to think that learning just meant studying. That was hard enough work. Today I'm finding that learning can be a lot harder than just studying."

Stevie and Carole knew exactly what she meant. They also knew that the hardest part probably wasn't over yet. They still had to face Max and Carole still had to face her father.

The decision was made. Samson was perfectly groomed. There could be no more delays. The three of them packed up Stevie's grooming gear and went to face the music in Max's office.

Max was there and so were the parent volunteers. The girls didn't like the idea of having a public audience, but the parents would all know soon enough. The hardest was the fact that Colonel Hanson was there. He smiled brightly at Carole. She hated to think how much she was about to hurt him.

"Max, there's something we have to tell you," Lisa began. While Lisa didn't know very much about hitching a pony to a cart, she knew a lot about explaining things clearly. She first described what had happened to each of their sets of study sheets and how the three of them found themselves at Carole's house without anything to study from. Then Carole took over. She spoke to Max, but her words were for her father.

"We didn't mean to be snooping or anything. It was just that we needed the study sheets and I knew Dad had put them on his desk. It never occurred to any of us that what the parent volunteers got from you was any different from what the pony clubbers had gotten."

"We just didn't know," Stevie said, taking over. "We made copies and we got to work. We've been working very hard, too. You can test us if you want. But we've been working on the wrong thing—or maybe it was the right thing, but anyway, we figured out that it was the wrong thing to do."

Lisa finished for them. "We're sorry, Max. We really are. We didn't mean to do this. For a little while after we discovered it, it seemed like a great thing, but in the end we know it's just not right. We need to learn everything there is to know about horses—not just what we're going to be tested on."

Colonel Hanson stood by the door of Max's office. His face didn't reveal anything. Max sat down and blew a chestful of air out through his pursed lips. Nobody said anything for a few minutes.

"You know what this means, don't you?" Max asked.

"Disqualified? Are we out?" Carole asked. She didn't want to miss the Know-Down, but even more than that, she didn't want to have to tell Cam about it all.

"No, I don't think so," Max said. "I suspect you three have been working very hard. In fact, judging by what else I've seen today, I suspect you've been working on the Know-Down material only." He glanced at Lisa. She looked at the floor. "No, what it means is that I'm going to have to make up new questions."

"It's going to be a lot more work and we're really sorry," said Stevie.

"I don't mind the work," Max said. "What I mind is that I thought I had made the meanest, sneakiest, and toughest questions possible out of that material on the study sheets. Now I have to be meaner, sneakier, and tougher—all because of you."

"You're very good at it," Stevie said. Then she realized that that might not sound like much of a compliment. She tried to soften it. "I mean, it takes one to know one," she told him.

He smiled weakly. Then he stood up. "Back to the drawing board," he said. "Now get out of here. I've got a lot of work to do. And so do you."

The girls shared a feeling that was hard to describe when they left Max's office. They felt awful because they knew they'd let Max down—and Colonel Hanson, too. They felt worried because they knew there were just a few days until the Know-Down and there was a lot to learn from the study sheets that they hadn't learned from the question-and-answer pages and they all wanted to do very well. And there was another feeling, too. They all felt relieved because they knew that, hard as it was, and as much trouble as they were causing, they felt better being honest about what had happened.

Carole and her father walked behind Lisa and Stevie. Nobody was talking. There was too much thinking going on. It took Carole only a minute to pick up her backpack from the locker area and she met her father in the car. She pulled the door closed and prepared for a long drive home.

Colonel Hanson started up the engine and the journey began.

"I'm sorry, Dad," Carole said. "I didn't mean to do it. I just didn't think—"

"I know you didn't think." The irritation was clear in his voice.

"I really *am* sorry," she repeated.

"I know you are, honey," he said more softly. "I know you didn't mean to do it. I always knew you didn't mean to. Almost, anyway. At first, I wasn't sure."

Always?

"You knew?"

"Sure, I did," he said. "From the moment I saw that the papers had been moved on my desk."

"And you didn't say anything?"

"What was I going to say? It was up to you to say something, not me. I knew you would, too."

"You did?"

"Of course I did. You're my daughter. You know right from wrong. Sometimes it might take you a while to figure out which is which, but I knew you'd come through."

Carole was simply stunned. Then another thought occurred to her.

"Did you think we were cheating?" she asked.

"I knew what you were up to," he said. "You broke the rules the moment you decided to take papers off my desk. The fact that you didn't know how much you were cheating is just a question of degree. What I was always sure of was that you'd come clean—only I didn't know when."

Carole didn't know what to say. Her father seemed to have an infinite capacity to surprise her. It made her love him all the more.

"Thanks, Dad," she said.

"For what?"

"For trusting me when I didn't deserve it."

He took her hand and squeezed it. "That's what dads are for," he said.

They rode the rest of the way home without talking. Carole mulled over all the events of the day. She'd learned a lot. Mostly, like Lisa, she'd learned that learning itself could involve a lot more than just studying hard. Some lessons were tougher than others. Today had been full of those.

"WHAT ARE THE five major internal parasites?" Carole asked Stevie. The three girls were sitting on bales of hay in the feed room, trying, once again, to make up for lost time.

Stevie grimaced. "Why do you always ask me that question? It's so disgusting to even think about those things."

"It's even more disgusting if you're a horse infested with them," Carole said. "Then you'd really want your owner to know."

"All right. Here goes: botflies, bloodworms, pinworms, intestinal worms, and stomach worms. But don't ask me how you know when your horse has them. It's more than I can handle."

"I won't," Carole promised. "That's what I'm going to ask Lisa."

Lisa was ready. "For botflies, you can spot the eggs on the horse's coat. For the other ones, major symptoms are weight loss, a potbelly, lethargy, tail rubbing, diarrhea, and coughing. But I agree with Stevie. Those things are just disgusting and the best way to cope with them is not to get them at all."

"How do you do that?" Carole asked. It wasn't an idle question. It was the next set of information on the sheet.

"Mainly cleanliness. If there isn't a lot of manure around, then the parasites can't breed and you break their life cycle. Also, have horses, especially young ones, eat from a manger that isn't on the ground where parasites breed. Keep the feed areas dry and the horses clean."

"Very good," said Carole. "But don't forget to have the horses checked and wormed regularly by a vet."

"Can we move on to something nicer?" Stevie asked.

Carole nodded. "Let's talk about equitation." She and Cam had been talking about it last night. She wanted to be sure to cover the subject with her friends, too.

Stevie sighed with relief as they continued their work.

The Saddle Club had been working very hard over the last few days to be sure they would know as much as possible at the Know-Down tomorrow. Stevie had talked to Phil the night before and it was clear that he'd been studying, too. He'd managed to drop a couple of rather obscure facts on her, like the place where the first three-day event was ever held in England (Badminton). Stevie's first reaction had been to wonder why anybody cared. Her second reaction was to wonder what other obscure information Phil might have mastered that would be just the thing to put him over the top in the Know-Down. The result of that was that she now knew that the three-day event had taken place in 1949. What she still hadn't figured out was who cared.

"Name the parts of a hoof visible on the underside of a shod hoof," Carole said to Lisa.

"The sole, the frog, and I think there's something else, but I can't remember what it is."

"Stevie?"

"The bars."

"The bars, the bars, the bars. Sole, frog, and bars,"

Lisa said, trying to recite the names so she'd remember them forever—or at least until tomorrow afternoon. She needed a memory trick. Stevie had one for her.

"I've got it. Remember that you want to stay out of the bar that serves filet of sole and frog legs," Stevie suggested. "It's not a place you want to go to while your horse is getting new shoes."

"I think that's longer and more complicated than remembering sole, frog, and bars."

"Whatever," Stevie said.

The girls continued working until they each thought facts would be floating out of their ears. Finally when their minds were fully stuffed with everything there was to know about horses, they all went home.

It didn't stop there, though. Stevie spent the rest of the afternoon and evening trying desperately to memorize every obscure fact Phil might know that she didn't. Lisa worked on everything she thought Stevie and Carole already knew because they'd been riding so much longer than she had. And Carole tried to master everything she thought was most important for a good rider, trainer, breeder, and vet to know.

That night Carole called Cam. She always enjoyed talking about horses and she always liked talking with Cam. Talking about horses *with* Cam was a great combination. Together, they went over some of the study sheets. Carole tested Cam and then Cam tested Carole. Carole thought they both did pretty well. It was a nice thought that helped her fall asleep easily.

WHEN CAROLE WOKE up the next morning, it took a minute for her to remember why she had butterflies in her stomach. Then it came to her. This was The Day. It was the Know-Down, but it was also the day that Cam was coming to Horse Wise. They had talked a lot—including last night—but the last time she had seen him was when they'd competed against one another at a horse show and now they would be competing in the Know-Down. That wasn't what was on her mind about him, though. What she was really thinking about was what a nice boy he was, how great he was with horses, and how good-looking, too. No wonder she had butterflies in her stomach!

Carole hopped out of bed, washed up, tidied her room, and got dressed quickly. Since she hoped to be able to ride with Cam after Horse Wise, she put on her riding clothes. She took an extra amount of time with her hair. She wanted to look her best.

Carole and her father arrived at Pine Hollow right before Cam's mother dropped him off. Carole felt a delightful little tingle when she saw him. She admitted to herself that she'd been nervous about meeting him face-to-face again, but once he arrived, she knew there wasn't anything to be nervous about. She was glad he was there. He was going to enjoy the day as much as she was.

Stevie was waiting for Phil to arrive. She waved cheerfully at Cam and Carole and then Carole took Cam on a tour of the stable.

"I've been studying those sheets you mailed me," Cam said as they walked around. "I hope I'll do okay."

"I'm sure you will," Carole assured him. "You know so much more than I do anyway."

"You think so?" He seemed genuinely surprised. "It seems to me that you know a lot more than *I* do, not the other way around."

Carole hadn't expected that at all. She smiled with pleasure, then said politely, "Well, what matters is to know enough to take good care of the horses." They both agreed on that.

In another part of the stable, Stevie was quizzing Phil. "What Olympics inspired the first three-day event in England?" she asked.

He grinned at her. There was a twinkle in his eye. "I want you to know that I know the answer to that. But I'm not going to tell you because I think you *don't*

106

know the answer and you're just trying to worm it out of me so you'll know, too."

Stevie was in a quandary. She did know the answer. But maybe Phil *didn't* know it and he was just trying to get her to tell him. Then she started laughing. The possibility that Max would ask such a silly question was just about zero. She continued with the game.

"Of course I know," she said. "But you're not going to get me to do *your* work." She looked at him and smiled brightly. One of the things Stevie liked the very most about Phil was that they understood a lot of things about each other without having to explain. Teasing each other was lots of fun.

Stevie took Phil's hand. "Come on," she said. "Let's go to the tack room where we can talk a little bit. I think you could use some brushing up on the three main types of coughing in horses."

"Oh, wow," Phil said. "I can hardly wait. Then can we do external parasites?"

"Definitely!"

In another part of the stable, Lisa was by herself. She'd seen Phil and Cam and she'd said hello. Both Carole and Stevie had invited her to come be with them and she knew they'd meant it, but she also knew it was a good time for Stevie and Carole to be with their boyfriends. Besides, she had something she wanted to do. She wanted to visit with the mare. She'd been so busy studying for the Know-Down that she'd almost forgotten the mare who she'd thought was going to have her foal two weeks before. Lisa shook her head. How little she seemed to know!

The mare raised her head anxiously when Lisa approached. She laid her ears back and then flicked them up again. Her tail swished. She was anxious, just the same way she had been two weeks ago. Lisa held her hand out in greeting. The mare ignored it. That was odd. A horse used to being around people usually wanted to sniff an offered hand, particularly if there was any reason to think that hand might hold some sugar or a carrot.

"It's okay, girl," Lisa told the mare. "I don't have anything for you anyway." She reached to pat the horse on her neck.

The mare stepped back from the pat.

Lisa looked at her watch. It was five minutes to ten. The Horse Wise meeting was about to start. She said good-bye and left the mare, who seemed as uninterested in Lisa's departure as she had been in her arrival.

"Horse Wise, come to order!"

There was a rustle of excitement and then quiet. Max welcomed everybody to the open meeting and then asked all the members to introduce themselves to the visitors. Three other Horse Wise members had invited friends to come to the meeting, so there were almost thirty young riders in the room.

Max explained the rules of the Know-Down.

"There are a lot of different ways you can do this, but here's how we're going to do it. I've made you into teams. There are seven teams of four members. I've tried to balance the teams so that they will all be relatively equal in riding experience."

That meant that he'd split up The Saddle Club. The girls knew it and were disappointed, but it was sort of a compliment. It meant that Max knew they had a lot of experience and he was pretty sure that they'd been working extra hard to do well to make up for causing him trouble, and he thought that if they were one team it wouldn't be fair to others. When Max named the teams, they learned that Stevie and Phil were on one team, Carole and Cam were on another, and Lisa was on a team with May. May seemed so happy about that that Lisa couldn't be upset about the fact that she'd been separated from her best friends. Each team had been named after one of the stable's horses. Carole's team was "Barq," Stevie's was "Topside," and Lisa's was "Comanche." Within the team, each player was assigned a number and the questions would go from team to team, number by number, so that the number one Barq player would answer a question, then the number one Topside player, then the number one Comanche player, and so on. When all the number ones had answered a question, it would be the number twos' turns. It seemed complicated, but Lisa was pretty sure she'd get the hang of it.

"All right, here we go," Max announced. "As I explained to most of you earlier, each question has an assigned value. You get to choose the level of difficulty —from one to four. If you get it right, you get it all right. If you get any of it wrong, you get it all wrong and the next person up will finish the question, having the benefit of knowing what was right and what was wrong about your answer. The disadvantage there is that the next person has to answer the level of difficulty chosen by the person who got it wrong. Everything clear?" The riders nodded. "Are you ready?"

"Ready!" they called out.

The Know-Down began.

Most of the riders wanted to start with pretty easy questions.

"What is a 'hand'?"

"Four inches."

"What side of the horse do you generally mount and dismount on?"

"Left."

"How do you change diagonals at a rising trot?"

"Sit two beats."

Then it was Stevie's turn. She decided to try for more and asked for a three-pointer.

"Where is the Spanish riding school?"

This was a trick question. If it had been a one-point question, it was possible that the answer might be

Spain, but as a three-point question, it couldn't be an easy answer. Stevie scrunched her eyebrows in thought. Then it came to her.

"Austria," she said.

"Yes," said Max.

"Nice," said Phil, and he clapped her on the back. Stevie actually blushed. Lisa saw it. She looked around to see if anybody else noticed. Nobody else seemed to. There was, however, an odd look on one person's face and that was Veronica's. The look was confusion. That was not an emotion Veronica usually either had or showed. Lisa wondered what she was confused about. She didn't have time to wonder for long, though, because it was her turn.

"Two points, please," she said, feeling bold.

"What steps should be taken to prevent tetanus?"

"Vaccination," she said. Then she paused. Was there something else? The question asked for "steps," not "step." She decided it needed more answer than she'd given. "There are a lot of things you can do to minimize exposure to tetanus, like cleaning stalls and the stable area, but wherever there are horses, there is tetanus, so horses should be vaccinated regularly, beginning at three or four months of age. Mares should be vaccinated before foaling so that the babies have immunity from her when they are born and any horse

112

who gets a puncture wound should be vaccinated with an antitoxin. In addition, all riders and anybody who works around horses should be immunized regularly. Is that enough answer?"

There was a moment of quiet. Lisa wondered what she'd done wrong. It turned out she hadn't done anything wrong.

"It's enough answer," Max assured her. "In fact, I think it was a four-point answer to a two-point question, so that's what I'm going to give you. Nice work, Lisa. And anyone else can earn extra points that way, too."

Lisa's teammates gave her high fives.

The next person up was Veronica. "Two points," she said. That made sense. Veronica was pretty smart about horses. She shouldn't begin with a one-point question.

"What should be your first action if your horse refuses his feed and appears dull and listless?" Max asked.

Lisa thought that was an easy question and should have been a one-pointer. If a rider suspected a horse was ill—and those were certainly signs of illness—the first thing to do was to check the horse's temperature.

"Call the vet," Veronica said. Lisa stifled a snicker. Veronica thought everything having to do with horses, except the actual riding, was something she had to get somebody else to do. Naturally, *she* would call the vet.

"Wrong," Max said. The question went to someone else who answered it correctly.

Then it was Cam's turn. He asked for a two-pointer as well.

"What are three places for feeling a horse's pulse?"

"Under and inside of the jawbone; in the cheek— that's above and behind the eye; and on the inside of the foreleg, by the knee."

"Good," Max said.

Phil then also asked for a two-point question.

"On a double rein, what are the two reins called and what's the difference between them?"

Phil had to think for a minute. "The bridoon and the bit reins. The bridoon is wider and longer."

"Good," said Max. He was smiling, obviously pleased that his riders and their guests had worked so hard and learned so much.

"You know, I have to say something. You all have obviously been working very hard and you're probably sitting there thinking that it's wonderful that you're doing well in this Know-Down, but the fact is, what you've worked on over these last two weeks *isn't* just for the Know-Down; it's for the horses and it's for life. Good job."

Everybody seemed proud of what Max was saying, but there were three girls in the group who thought they understood it better than anybody else. It had been their love of horses more than anything that had made them confess their mistake. They had never regretted their honesty. Now they were downright proud of it.

There wasn't time to think about that much, though, because the questions continued at a rapid pace. Some of the riders made mistakes, of course. Not everybody got everything. Stevie was stumped by a two-pointer that asked what the usual angle was between the wall of a normal foot and the ground. She forgot that it was fifty degrees. Lisa was pleased that *she* remembered, because the question came to her when Stevie missed it and she got it right.

Right after Lisa, Veronica was stumped by a two-pointer.

"To which of the three straps on a saddle should the two buckles of a girth be fastened?"

Veronica had no idea at all and her blank look said everything. In a way, it wasn't surprising, since she never did her own girth if she could talk somebody else into doing it, but the fact was it was a pretty basic question and she should have known. In addition to that, it was right on the study sheets.

May took the question and answered it correctly. "The two front or the first and third," she said.

"Good," Max praised her.

Carole was puzzled. Veronica's mistakes didn't make much sense. Veronica was a pretty good rider and should have picked up some information along the way, although people did have a tendency to forget information they didn't use. But recently, she'd seen Veronica with study sheets. Also Veronica had seemed confident of her ability to do well in the Know-Down and that could only mean she'd been working on it. Certainly, the girl had known she couldn't get a stable hand to do this for her! There was something very odd going on with Veronica and Carole didn't know what it was.

It seemed that Veronica didn't know either, but what she did to remedy the situation was to start asking for one-point questions.

"What should you do as you approach a horse?"

Veronica thought for a moment. "Speak to him?"

"Yes," Max said.

Her question the next time around was even easier. "How many beats are there in a canter?"

"Three," she answered confidently.

116

"Very good!" Max said. He was being a little sarcastic, which was unlike him, but it was clear now to more than just Carole that Veronica was somehow totally unprepared for this Know-Down and nobody knew why that was. If she was so unprepared, why had she come at all?

The answer to that question came to Carole on the next round. The person before Veronica, Adam Levine, chose a three-point question.

"Name the parts of the mouth and head affected by a bit and the other parts of the bridle."

Adam grimaced. Then he took a deep breath. He obviously didn't know the answer off the top of his head, but he was going to try.

"The tongue, the roof of the mouth, and the nose?"

"Good start, but not enough. Who's up next? Veronica?"

Veronica stood up. "The lips and corners of the mouth, the bars of the mouth, the tongue, the roof of the mouth, the poll, the chin-groove, and the nose," she said, and she sat down.

"Very good," Max said. He seemed a little surprised, but pleased.

Carole was surprised, too. There was something extremely familiar about the words she'd just heard recited flawlessly by Veronica and Carole puzzled for a minute to recall just why they were so familiar. Then it came to her. What was familiar about them was that that was one of the questions she and her friends had been studying from the question-and-answer sheet. It was also by far the toughest question Veronica had gotten right. There had to be a reason.

Then a possible explanation came to Carole. Veronica *had* been studying hard. She'd been studying very hard, but she hadn't been using the study sheets; she'd only been using the question-answer pages The Saddle Club had gotten from Colonel Hanson's desk. The reason Veronica had seemed so confident before the Know-Down had begun was that she knew the answers to everything she'd studied, but those weren't the questions Max was mostly asking.

Carole wanted to think about this more, but she didn't have time right then. The Barq team was up again and it was Cam's turn.

"Four points," he said. Carole took in a little gasp of air. Four points meant it would be a very hard question. Could he do it?

Max flipped pages. "All right," he said. "In a dressage arena, name the letters, clockwise, starting at C."

Carole groaned inwardly. There was no logical pattern that she'd ever been able to determine to

118

the points on the side of a dressage arena, identified by letter. Cam would never get this, she was sure, and the puzzled look on his face told her she was right.

Then he spoke. "Large or small?" he asked.

"Small. I'll give you two extra points if you can also do large."

Cam did. "C, M, B, F, A, K, E, and H make up the small arena. The large is C, M, R, B, P, F, A, K, V, E, S, and H. In the small arena, the letters down the center are G, X, and D. In the large, they are G, I, X, L, and D."

"And I guess I have to give you another two points for doing the center letters. Nice job!"

Everybody there was impressed and clapped for Cam. Carole was so proud of him, she could barely contain herself. She looked around the room at all her riding friends, smiling happily for her. That included almost everybody there. The one exception—the one person who wasn't smiling—was Veronica. It was almost her turn again.

"Veronica?" Max asked.

"One point," she grunted.

"What do we call a horse who has a brown coat with black mane and tail?"

"Bay," she shot back.

"Very good! And on that note, we'll have a brief break. Take five. Juice is on the table behind you."

Carole stood up and turned around to get some juice. When she did so, she found herself face-to-face with Veronica diAngelo, who was glaring straight at her.

"You did that on purpose!" Veronica snarled. "You left those papers there and then you didn't tell me when you got caught cheating, just so you could make me look bad!"

"I—what?" Carole said.

"Well, I'm tired of your game and I won't play it anymore!"

Veronica spun on her heel, marched over to Max, said something vague about a stomachache, and went home.

"What was *that* all about?" Stevie asked Carole.

"I'm not sure, but I'm working on it and I think I like it," Carole said.

"Anything that gets Veronica out of the room I'm in is good news," said Stevie.

"Especially if she's angry at us," added Lisa.

"What are you three talking about?" Cam asked, handing Carole a paper cup filled with apple juice.

"Saddle Club business," Carole said vaguely. "We'll

fill you in later, once I'm sure I understand it." Her mind was racing so fast that she didn't notice how quickly the time passed.

"Horse Wise, come to order!"

The Know-Down began again.

"OKAY, CAROLE, WHAT *was* that all about?" Stevie demanded as the five successful Know-Down players tried to figure out how they would celebrate their successes at the end of the Horse Wise meeting. May Grover was with them, so that made six. They'd all done well and were feeling almost giddy. The first success to be celebrated had to be overwhelming Veronica. If only they knew how they'd done it. Carole thought she had the answer.

"It was when the pony got loose," Carole said. "It had to be then. Remember?"

The girls tried to recall what had happened that day.

"The three of us were sitting in the empty stall next to Garnet. We didn't really know it, but Veronica was with Garnet and she must have been listening to us quiz one another."

"Sure, but how did she know what was going on?"

"She must have realized from what we were saying that we weren't using the same study sheets we'd all been given. After all, she'd been studying from the sheets. She knew the format was different. She must have figured out that we had the real thing. "She knew even before we did."

Lisa nodded. It was becoming clear to her. "Sure!" she said. "If her father were one of the volunteers, you can bet she would have talked him into giving her a set of the actual questions. She would, naturally, think you'd do the same thing!"

Carole looked alarmed.

"Don't worry," Stevie reassured her. "Nobody else would think something like that. But how did Veronica get the sheets?"

Carole went on. She'd figured this part out. "There we were, quizzing one another, when Nickel got loose. We all jumped up and ran after him. It probably took us about a half an hour, maybe more. I was in such a hurry to get Nickel that I forgot to put the question-and-answer sheets in my pocket. Obviously Miss

123

Snoop spotted them, took them to Mrs. Reg's office, used the copying machine, and put them back. When I went back to find them, I noticed that they were in a different corner of the stall, but I didn't think anything of it. I also noticed that the stall door was open. If I'd stopped to think about it, I would have known she'd been there because she's the only one around who *always* leaves doors open and gates unlatched. Anyway, that's how the deed was done."

"And Veronica's goose was cooked." Stevie sighed contentedly. "It was wonderful!"

"What are you three talking about?" Cam asked.

"The fall of Miss Veronica diAngelo," Stevie said.

Carole wouldn't have put it so poetically, but she had to agree. "I'll explain it to you later," she told Cam. "For now, trust me, it's good news. So, in the meantime, tell me how it is that you know all the letters around a dressage arena."

"I'd be glad to explain it in detail," Cam teased. "But I'd rather have you show me the trails at Pine Hollow. Didn't you say something about taking a ride?"

Carole smiled. She was afraid he'd forgotten. "I did," Carole said. "And I've also got Max's permission for you to take Comanche. The tack room's this way."

She offered him her hand. He took it and they walked off.

Phil cleared his throat. "Um, speaking of guided tours," he said to Stevie. "Weren't you going to show me the new grain shed?"

"New grain shed?" May asked. "There isn't a new grain shed."

"Well, then, the old grain shed," he said.

"This way," Stevie told him, and the two of them went off together.

"What does he want to see an old grain shed for?" May asked Lisa.

Lisa laughed. She put her arm around May's shoulders. "I don't think he much cares about the grain shed at all," she explained. "He just wants to be with Stevie for a while."

"Oh. Like alone?"

"Right, like alone," Lisa said.

"Got it. Don't you mind, though?"

"Mind?" Lisa asked.

"That your friends have got boyfriends that they're going to be alone with?" May did have a way of cutting right to the core of something.

Lisa thought about it for a few seconds. "Not really," she answered truthfully. "Sometime I'll have a boyfriend, too. But right now, I've got a friend and I have to ask her a favor."

"Go ahead," May said. "You can leave me." She seemed a little disappointed that Lisa was apparently going to leave her alone.

"No, you're the friend," said Lisa.

"Me? What's the favor?"

"I need help with something. I didn't learn anywhere near what I should have about harnesses and carts for our project. You did all the work. I got distracted by the Know-Down, which was important, but not so important that it was okay to let you down."

"Me?"

"Yeah, you. Anyway, will you show me how to hitch up a pony to a cart?"

"Me?"

"Yes, you, my friend, my smart, hard-working, pony-hitching friend."

"Well, sure," May said. "Now?"

"When better?"

"Okay." May shrugged and led the way to where the harness was stored.

The girls took the harness off its hooks and laid it out on the floor. May began methodically naming all the parts and explaining them as she went. Lisa listened very carefully. This time she was actually learning it.

At the point when May got to the parts of the harness that actually hitched the pony to the cart, the door to the storeroom opened and Max walked in.

"What are you two up to?" he asked.

"It's the Big Sis/Little Sis project, Max, don't you remember?" May asked him.

"Well, more like a Little Sis/Big Sis project," Lisa said, and then Max understood. He smiled and left them alone.

May finished her explanation and the two girls put the harness back up on its hooks. Lisa knew that she would need to spend a little more time studying before she could remember all the names of all the parts of the harness, but she also knew she'd learned the basics from May and could take it from there by herself. And she would, too.

The two of them left the room. May's mother was picking her up in a few minutes and she had to get her bag from the locker area first. She turned to go left to the locker area. Lisa turned right.

"Where are you going?" May asked.

"To check on the mare," Lisa said. "Want to say hello?"

"Sure," May agreed.

Together, the two of them walked over to the stall. Lisa expected to hear more of the agitated stomping of the excited mare, but there was only quiet rustling. The mare stood calmly. Lisa was glad she was more relaxed now.

As they neared the stall, Lisa noticed another noise, sort of a snorting and thumping, but it wasn't coming from the mare. It was coming from a brand-new foal! There, standing next to her mother, was a little filly with a shiny brown coat and a little brush for a tail.

"Oh!" May said, her voice filled with wonder. Lisa thought that was just the right reaction and couldn't have said it better herself. The two of them gazed at the perfect baby horse.

In time they were joined by a quiet, admiring circle of young riders.

Max came and stood with them, too. "There's something very special about a newborn foal, and no matter how many times I've seen it, it's always special."

"It's a new start," Lisa agreed. "A whole new life, with no past, a whole new promise."

"Yes," he agreed. "That's just what it is. A promise. And I think that's what this filly should be named, too. Welcome to the world, Promise," he said.

When the other riders had gone, picked up by their parents or walking home on their own, Lisa remained by the foal and the mare, watching with wonder. She was struck by the liveliness of the foal and the calmness of the mare and that reminded her of the agitated state of the mare over the last few weeks. That, in turn, reminded her of her certainty that the foal was going to arrive two weeks earlier when she'd first noticed the mare's edginess. Then the mare had been edgy this morning, too, and this morning it apparently *had* meant that the mare was about to foal.

So what was the difference? Lisa didn't know the answer and doubted she was going to learn it watching the baby playing now. She did remember that Judy had seemed certain two weeks ago that the foal wasn't going to arrive for about two weeks and Judy had been right. Maybe the only thing Lisa could learn about this was that sometimes other people knew better than she did and she'd be smart to pay attention. Maybe that wasn't a bad lesson.

14

IT HAD BEEN a perfect day as far as the Saddle Club girls were concerned. The whole day was spent at Pine Hollow working with, riding, and learning about horses. By the time dusk came and Phil and Cam had gone home, Lisa, Stevie, and Carole were all nicely tired and content.

"I think it's time for a Saddle Club meeting," Carole said.

"TD's?" Stevie asked. They hadn't been to their favorite ice cream parlor in a while.

"No, I don't want to leave here, yet," said Lisa. "Let's go sit on the hillside overlooking the paddocks."

It sounded to the girls like the perfect way to end the perfect day.

The three of them sat down together.

"Did you and Cam have a nice ride?" Lisa asked.

"Oh, yes," Carole said. "It was great. I showed him my favorite path through the woods—"

"To the creek?" Carole nodded. "Did you sit on the rock and soak your feet?"

"We sat on the rock. It's still too cold for foot soaking. More like foot chilling! It was just awfully nice to be able to share a place I love with a friend. What did you do while we were riding?"

Lisa told her about working on the harness and hitching with May. Because Stevie and Carole were her friends, they knew they didn't have to make any comments about what a good idea that was. They just plain understood.

"Max asked me to be a Big Sis at the next meeting," Stevie said.

"You're supposed to teach somebody mischief?" Lisa teased. Everybody knew that mischief was Stevie's strongest subject.

"Nope. We're supposed to bone up on nutrition and feeding schedules. Things like that."

"Who's your Little Sis?"

"Make that 'Bro,' " said Stevie. "It's Craig Watson

—you know that weird little boy who is always making trouble in class, talking and joking?"

Carole and Lisa thought that was a good description of Craig. It also seemed like a fairly apt description of somebody else they knew. "Birds of a feather!" Carole declared.

"Right," Stevie agreed. "We'll never learn anything!"

Lisa didn't agree. "You could be surprised by how much you learn when you're supposed to be the teacher."

"We'll see," said Stevie.

They were quiet then for a few minutes, watching the sun settle into the clouds above the hills to the west. Then there was a sharp thumping sound down by the stable. The girls looked. The paddock door was opened by Judy Barker. She stood aside and waited. The girls waited, too. Then, while they watched, the filly, now officially dubbed Promise, took her first steps into the fresh air of Virginia. She paused, put her nose up to the breeze, sniffed, and nodded. Then, delicate and prancing, she seemed to dance across the paddock. She stopped and turned. The mare stepped toward her protectively. The filly responded immediately by returning to her mother's side and nuzzled at the mare's belly for a snack.

Judy invited the mare and her baby to return to the stable then. The door closed and the magical moment was over.

"The perfect end to a perfect day," said Carole, sighing happily.

"Any day in which we find a way to let Veronica make a public fool of herself *is* a perfect day," Stevie agreed.

"I just thought of something," Lisa said.

"What?" asked Carole.

"Which team won the Know-Down?"

The girls looked at one another. They had no idea what the answer was. They'd all enjoyed competing so much that they hadn't paid any attention to the score at the end.

"I think I know, though," Stevie said. Her friends looked at her and she continued. "Personally, I think The Saddle Club won it."

"I agree," Carole said.

"See, that's the thing I love about The Saddle Club," Lisa said. "When we put our minds to it, we can solve any problem at all."

"Even ones we create ourselves," said Carole.

They gave one another high fives and then sat back to watch the rest of the sunset.

133

BONNIE BRYANT is the author of more than fifty books for young readers, including novelizations of movie hits such as *Teenage Mutant Ninja Turtles®* and *Honey, I Blew Up the Kid*, written under her married name, B. B. Hiller.

Ms. Bryant began writing The Saddle Club in 1986. Although she had done some riding before that, she intensified her studies then and found herself learning right along with her characters, Stevie, Carole, and Lisa. She claims that they are all much better riders than she is.

Ms. Bryant was born and raised in New York City. She lives in Greenwich Village with her two sons.

T · H · E

SADDLE CLUB

A blue-ribbon series by Bonnie Bryant

Stevie, Carole and Lisa are all very different, but they *love* horses!
The three girls are best friends at Pine Hollow Stables, where they
ride and care for all kinds of horses. Come to Pine Hollow and get
ready for all the fun and adventure that comes with being 13!

**Watch for other THE SADDLE CLUB books all year.
More great reading—and riding to come!**